SUMMER WITH A FRENCH SURGEON

BY
MARGARET BARKER

First published in Great Britain 2012
by Mills & Boon, an imprint of Harlequin (UK) Limited.
Large Print edition 2012
Harlequin (UK) Limited, Eton House,
18-24 Paradise Road, Richmond, Surrey TW9 1SR

© Margaret Barker 2012

ISBN: 978 0 263 22479 5

Harlequin (UK) policy is to use papers that are natural, renewable and recyclable products and made from wood grown in sustainable forests. The logging and manufacturing process conform to the legal environmental regulations of the country of origin.

Printed and bound in Great Britain
by CPI Antony Rowe, Chippenham, Wiltshire

Margaret Barker has enjoyed a variety of interesting careers. A State Registered Nurse and qualified teacher, she holds a degree in French and Linguistics, and is a Licentiate of the Royal Academy of Music. As a full-time writer, Margaret says, 'Writing is my most interesting career, because it fits perfectly into family life. Sadly, my husband died of cancer in 2006, but I still live in our idyllic sixteenth-century house near the East Anglian coast. Our grown-up children have flown the nest, but they often fly back again, bringing their own young families with them for wonderful weekend and holiday reunions.'

Recent titles by the same author:

A FATHER FOR BABY ROSE
GREEK DOCTOR CLAIMS HIS BRIDE
THE FATHERHOOD MIRACLE

These books are also available in eBook format from www.millsandboon.co.uk

To my wonderful family, who give me continual love, inspiration and happiness.

CHAPTER ONE

EVER since she'd been tiny, Julia had always made a special point of trying to appear confident. Well, with three older brothers to boss her around she'd had to be tough to survive. Still, glancing around now at her fellow trainee surgeons, she felt decidedly nervous. Since her disastrous marriage to Tony—who'd done his best to destroy whatever confidence she'd had— her life had been an uphill struggle to even get back to how she'd felt as a teenager, competing against her brilliant medical-student and qualified brothers.

Coming here, to France, to further her surgical career was the first step on her long journey back to self-confidence. And, in fact, looking out of the taxi as she had been driven down the hill just now towards St Martin sur Mer, she'd been in seventh heaven as she'd absorbed the wonderful scenery spread out in front of her. The stunning view had made her forget any apprehension she'd had about taking this big step.

She'd found herself overwhelmed with nostalgia as she'd seen the undulating sand dunes spilling down onto the beach and behind them the small, typically French hotels, cafés *tabac*, restaurants, shops and houses clustered near the high-tech hospital. She'd felt the excitement she'd known as a child when her French mother and English father, both doctors, had brought the whole family here for a couple of weeks every summer holiday.

She brought her thoughts back to the present as the eminent professor of orthopaedic surgery strode into the room. She caught her breath. Wow! Bernard Cappelle looked much younger than she'd expected and very…handsome? She paused, surprised by the turn of her wicked thoughts. It had been a very long time since she'd noticed any man in that way.

He was more than handsome, he was charismatic. Yes, that was more like it. He was oozing the sort of confidence she longed to acquire. Well, maybe, just maybe in another ten years, when she was an eminent surgeon, she would stride into a room and silence would descend as her students stared in awe at their professor of surgery, as was happening now with the great Bernard Cappelle.

If she hadn't made a concrete decision to hold off relationships since Tony had bled her dry of all desire for emotional commitment of any kind she would have allowed herself to fancy Bernard Cappelle.

In your dreams, girl! No chance! She wouldn't let herself even fantasise about him. Good! That meant she could concentrate on making the most of the six-month course without wasting her energy on emotional dreams about an unattainable man who wouldn't even notice her.

The awesome man cleared his throat as he looked around the assembled doctors. Ah, so he was possibly a bit nervous? At least that meant he had a human side.

'Hello, and welcome, ladies and gentlemen. I hope that...'

Bernard Cappelle began by welcoming them to the Hopital de la Plage, which would be their place of study and work for the six-month course. He explained they would study an orthopaedic operation theoretically before they moved on to the practical aspect of observing and assisting in Theatre. They would also be expected to assist with the pre- and post-operative care of the patients and also work in *Urgences*, the accident and emergency department, on occasion if required.

Julia took notes but realised soon enough that she'd read most of this in the brochure she'd studied carefully before applying. So she allowed herself to study the man who was to lead them all to the final exams, which would give them a prestigious qualification that would be a definite help to her in her desire to become a first-class orthopaedic surgeon.

She sat back in her hard and uncomfortable chair, probably designed to keep students awake. There were ten students on the course, Dr Cappelle explained. He'd chosen them from their CVs and was confident from their qualifications and experience that they were all going to give the next six months one hundred per cent of their available effort. He paused for a moment and his eyes swept the room before alighting on Julia in the front row.

'Are you happy for me to speak French all the time, Dr Montgomery?' he asked in heavily accented but charming English.

She was taken aback by suddenly being the centre of attention. Everyone was waiting for her reply. She swallowed hard. 'Yes, yes, of course. My mother is French, my father English, so I'm bilingual.'

'Then if you are happy I will speak in French...' He went on to explain that he was much happier when speaking French. 'And you are not intimidated by being the only lady in the class?'

She sat up straight, trying to look bigger than she actually was. 'Not at all. I was brought up with three brothers who did their best to intimidate me but without success.'

There was a scattering of sympathetic laughter. She was quaking in her shoes but making a valiant effort not to show it. She wished he would take his eyes off her and attention would focus on someone else.

'Excellent!'

A student sitting nearby spoke out in a clear distinct voice. 'Why is it, sir, that women orthopaedic surgeons are few and far between?'

Bernard Cappelle appeared to be giving the matter some thought. 'Good question. Could it be that the fairer sex are more delicate and possibly wary of taking on a profession that requires a certain amount of strength on occasions? What is your view, Dr Montgomery?'

'I have to say,' she continued boldly, forcing herself to display a confidence she didn't feel, 'I'm surprised to be the only woman on the course. I've never found, during my early career so far in orthopaedics, that being female is a disadvantage. When you're operating the patient is usually sedated in some way…I mean they're not likely to struggle with you or…'

Her voice trailed away as her depleted confidence ebbed and flowed.

The student who'd begun the discussion broke in. 'And there's always some hunky big, strong male doctor hovering around a fragile lady, hoping she'll ask for his help so that he can muscle in and…'

She missed the end of his sentence because the entire group was now laughing loudly. Ha, ha, very funny…she didn't think. She waited until the laughter died down before taking a deep breath and speaking in the clear, concise, correct French her well-spoken mother had always insisted she use.

'Gentlemen, you can be assured that I never take advantage of my so-called fragility. My brothers took me to judo classes when I was very young. I was awarded a black belt as soon as I was old enough to qualify and the skills I learned have often come in handy. So, as you can see, I only need to call for help when it's absolutely necessary.'

'Bravo!' Dr Cappelle said, admiration showing in his eyes. From her position in the front row she could see they were sensitive, a distinctive shade of hazel. Phew, she was glad she'd had to practise the art of being strong from an early age. Her show of pseudo-confidence was turning into the real thing, although she realised that had she known she would be the only woman on the course she might have hesitated before signing up.

Well, probably only hesitated for a short while. Looking around, she knew she could handle these young doctors, whatever they tried on. She'd learned a lot about men in the last few years. Basically, they were still boys, feeling as daunted as she was at the prospect of the exacting course they'd signed up to.

'I'm now going to give you a tour of the operating theatres we use here at the Hopital de la Plage. Some of them will be in use and we won't be able to go inside en masse. May I suggest you make a note of the areas you aren't able to see today so that you can find a more suitable time to inspect them at a later date?'

Before they all filed out, the professor asked them to call him Bernard. He said that he didn't hold with titles in a teaching situation, explaining that it was easier for him to get to know his students if there was always a warm atmosphere, especially in tutorials like today. He looked around the room as if to judge the collective reaction of his students to this unexpected statement.

There was a stunned silence. Julia felt slightly more at ease with the great man when he said that but as she glanced around the room she knew that her fellow students weren't taken in. Bernard Cappelle somehow managed to remain aloof even while he spoke. She sensed an aura of mystery surrounding him, which made him seem distant, brooding, definitely enigmatic, approachable in a professional situation but with caution. Yes, his students would call him Bernard because he'd requested they do so but at the same time they would be wary of him. So would she but for several reasons, some of them decidedly inadvisable given her past history!

Being in the front row, she went out first and found Bernard walking beside her. He seemed very tall. She wished she'd put her heels on but hadn't realised they were going to trek round the hospital.

'You don't mind if I call you Julia, do you?'

He had such a deep, sexy, mellifluous voice. She was going to have to be very firm with herself to eliminate any sign that she felt an attraction to him. There, she'd admitted it. Well, power plus charisma, plus a barely discernible twinkle in the eye, which undoubtedly accompanied a wicked sense of humour, all added up to a desirable package that she certainly wasn't going to attempt to unwrap. Bernard could teach her his professional skills and knowledge and that was all she wanted from him.

Besides, he was probably married, bound to have a stunning wife waiting for him at home. Although married men were often ready for a fling and flings were another thing totally off her agenda.

'Yes, you can call me Julia.' She didn't even smile, making it seem as if she was doing him a favour.

'Good.'

They were now going inside one of the theatres, which Bernard had told them was not in use that afternoon. There was gleaming, bright high-tech equipment everywhere she looked. She was really going to enjoy working in a place like this.

At the end of the afternoon tour Bernard took them down to the staff cafeteria, where the conversation drifted from the equipment they'd viewed and the endless possibilities of a teaching hospital of this calibre to their previous experience and what they hoped to get out of the course that would be relevant to their future careers.

Somehow she found herself next to Bernard again. She wondered if he felt he had to protect her from the attentions of her fellow students in spite of the fact that she'd made it quite clear she wanted to be treated in the same way as all the men on the course.

'So, do you think you're going to enjoy working here, Julia?'

'I don't know whether *enjoy* is quite the right word.' She took a sip of her coffee. 'I intend to get the most out of it but I realise it's going to be hard work.'

'You look like the sort of person who enjoys hard work—determined, tough, doesn't give up easily. From your CV you seem to have led a busy life both in and outside hospital. Am I right, Julia?'

She nodded. 'I suppose so—at least, that's what people have told me concerning my professional life. I've been focussed on my medical career throughout my adult life.'

'Did that give you enough time for your private life?'

'My private life? Well...'

She broke off. She wasn't going to notify her teacher that she'd come to the conclusion she had a serious flaw in her personality—her inability to handle her time outside the pursuit of her career. Especially in her inability to recognise a complete and utter swine when she thought she'd picked the man of her dreams. She turned her head away from him so that he wouldn't notice the misty, damp expression in her eyes that would give him an inkling of her intense vulnerability since the suffering Tony had inflicted on her.

Looking round the almost deserted cafeteria, she noticed that the majority of her fellow doctors were drifting out through the door, having been told that the rest of the day was theirs to orientate themselves around the hospital or do whatever they wanted.

She had been planning to escape back to the small study-bedroom she'd been assigned in the medical quarters and sort out her luggage. She felt that would be the safest option open to her now, instead of having a discussion about her least favourite subject.

She stood up. 'If you'll excuse me, Bernard,

I'm going to make use of this free time to get my room sorted out.'

It sounded trite to her own ears but the last thing she wanted so early in the course was to be interrogated by her boss on the delicate subject of her private life.

As he rose to his full height there was an enigmatic expression on his face. 'Of course, Julia.'

He escorted her to the door. She turned left towards the medical residents' quarters. He turned right towards the theatre block.

She walked swiftly down the corridor. At the entrance to the door to the residents' quarters she found one of her colleagues waiting for her. She recognised him as the one who'd had most to say for himself. Tall, dark and good looking in a rugged sort of way, very self-assured.

He smiled, displaying strong white teeth as he stretched out a hand towards her.

'Dominic,' he said, as he shook her hand in a firm grip.

She reclaimed her hand. 'Julia.'

'I know. Some of us are having an impromptu

meeting at the bar round the corner and we'd like you to join us if you could spare the time.'

'Well, my room needs sorting and—'

'Julia, we've all got things to do but…' He broke off and began speaking in English. 'All work and no play isn't good for you.'

She smiled at him. She needed to stop taking herself so seriously and it would be good to get to know her colleagues.

'OK. I'll come but I mustn't stay too long.'

'Don't worry. We're all in the same boat.'

'Ah, it's good to be outside in the fresh air.' Julia revelled in the warm early evening sunshine as they walked out through the hospital gates.

Across the road there were still families on the beach, children running into the sea, which she knew would still be a little chilly in the spring.

'Café Maurice Chevalier,' she read from the sign outside the café restaurant Dominic took her to.

She could see some of her fellow students grouped around a large table outside. Two of them were already pulling up another small table and a couple of chairs. There was a bottle of wine on the table. Someone poured her a glass. Dominic went inside to the bar, returning with another bottle and some more glasses.

Dominic went round the table, topping up wine glasses. They all raised their glasses to cries of '*Santé!*'

'Cheers!' said Dominic, proud of his English.

'Cheers!' everybody repeated, laughing loudly.

Names were bandied about and she managed to put names to faces. Pierre, Christophe, Daniel, Jacques, Gerard and Paul were the most vociferous. Dominic seemed to have been elected leader of the group. Julia was secretly glad she'd got brothers who'd shown her how to join in when she found herself in all-male company.

'This place was here when I was a child,' she said, during an unusually quiet moment. 'I used to sit outside and watch the sun going down with my parents and my brothers. It's good to be back here.'

'I should think it's good to escape from the attentions of our grumpy old tutor,' Dominic said. 'I saw him deep in conversation with you. How did he come across on a one-to-one basis?'

'To be honest, I don't know what to make of him. All I hope is that he's a good teacher.'

'Oh, he's a good teacher,' Dominic said vehemently. 'But he's a hard taskmaster. Apparently, he went through a difficult divorce and he's sorting out custody of his six-year-old son at the moment.'

'How do you know?' Pierre asked, screwing up his eyes against the glare of the setting sun.

Dominic grinned. 'I came here a week early to get the feel of the place. Unlike Julia, I've never been to this part of France before. I was born in Marseilles. I chatted up one of the nurses—'

Loud guffaws around the table greeted this.

'And found out a lot about Professor Grumpy. There's a rumour that he's going through a bad time at the moment, touchy about his divorce and tends to take it out on his students if they don't come up to scratch. But he's a brilliant surgeon and teacher, much admired by his colleagues.'

'Well, that's all I need to know,' Julia said, putting her hand over her glass as Christophe came round with another bottle.

'Ah, don't be too complacent,' Dominic told her. 'It's also rumoured that he doesn't think women make good surgeons.'

All eyes were on her now. She found herself filled with dread. Not only was she desperate to make a good impression on her new teacher but she was battling with an insane attraction towards him. Could it be true he didn't like women surgeons? So why had she been the only woman chosen for his exclusive course?

She looked out over the beach to the sand dunes at the corner of the bay, breathing slowly until the feeling of dread disappeared. She would cope. She would have to. She turned her head to look up at the magnificent hill behind them. She didn't want negative thoughts to spoil the beautiful sunset that was casting a glow over the hills, just as she remembered from her childhood.

She glanced round the table. 'My tutor in England told me I'm a good surgeon,' she said quietly. 'It's what I want to do with my life. And I'm not going to let a grumpy tutor spoil my career plans.'

A cheer went round the table. She felt she'd been accepted, just as her brothers' friends accepted her.

She stood up, smiling at her colleagues who had now become her friends. 'I've really enjoyed myself but I must go.'

'I'll come with you, escort you back.'

'No, you stay and have another drink, Dominic. It's not far.'

He pulled a wry face, but let her go off by herself.

She walked quickly, pausing as she went round the corner to look up at the sun dipping behind the hills. It had almost disappeared but a pink and mauve colour was diffusing over the skyline. She remembered how she'd once thought it was a miracle that the sun could disappear behind the hills and reappear from the depths of the sea in the morning. Her father had explained about the earth being round and so on but she'd still thought it was a miracle. Still did!

She turned her head and looked out at the darkening sea. There were fireflies dancing on the black waves, illuminating the scene. It was truly romantic, though not if you were all alone surrounded by strolling couples and families taking their children home to bed. She reminded herself that this was the life she'd now chosen, to ensure that she pursued her chosen career to the height of her destiny.

A smile flitted across her lips as she told herself to lighten up. It was a bit early to be having grand thoughts about her destiny.

Oh, yes, she was going to enjoy her evening now that she'd calmed her wicked thoughts and got herself back on the journey that she'd set herself. There would be time enough for romance, marriage, babies and everything else she wouldn't allow herself until she'd established her career.

CHAPTER TWO

Almost three weeks later Julia was sitting outside Bernard's office, waiting for her turn to have a one-on-one meeting with him about her progress to date. She was studying the printed sheets that Bernard had handed out at the last tutorial. It was difficult to believe that the first month of their course was almost over. The days had flown by during which they'd all been bombarded with work assignments, essays to write on the theories behind various orthopaedic operations and actual operations to observe in Theatre.

Whilst in Theatre they had to make copious notes, all of which needed to be written up in their own time. The notes then had to be transformed into a coherent observation of the operation, including their own comments and criticisms. These were emailed to Bernard as soon as possible. In no time at all they received an assessment of their work with much criticism from him. She knew she wasn't alone in being the recipient of his scathing comments.

They'd also undertaken sessions in the *Urgences* department, the French equivalent of Accident and Emergency, where they had to do minor operations and treatments on emergency cases, observed and assessed by the director of *Urgences*, Michel Devine. He in turn reported back to the twitchy Bernard.

When Dominic had told everybody that Bernard was reputed to be a hard taskmaster, he had been spot on! She'd been so naive three weeks ago. She hadn't believed she would have to work under such pressure.

Just at that moment Dominic arrived in the corridor and plonked himself down beside her.

'What time's your endurance test?'

She frowned at him. 'Shh. He'll hear you.'

'Don't care if he does. I feel like walking out. It's time he cut us some slack. We're all qualified and experienced doctors, for heaven's sake. Who does he think he is, treating us like—?'

The door opened. 'Good morning, Julia. Dominic,' their taskmaster said, glancing severely at Dominic.

Julia followed Bernard inside and sat down on the upright chair in front of the desk. She wasn't afraid of him, she told herself as he went round to the other side and glanced at the screen of his computer. She reckoned all the information on her was there. Everything she'd ever done since aspiring to take on this arduous course.

He looked across the desk at her and at last there was eye contact with him. She couldn't help the frisson of excitement that ran through her as she looked directly into those dark hazel eyes. Why was she being so perverse in finding herself attracted to this man who'd made the past three weeks such an endurance test for her?

'How are you finding the course, Julia?'

No smile, just that piercing stare that was causing shivers to run down her spine. Shivers she couldn't possibly analyse.

She took a deep breath. 'It's relentlessly tiring…but exceptionally interesting and frustrating at the same time.'

He frowned. 'In what way is it frustrating?'

'Well, you haven't yet let me loose in Theatre so I can do some actual surgery. I'm getting withdrawal symptoms from all this theorising.'

Was that a brief twitching of the lips or the beginnings of a contemptuous smile on his face? Whatever it was, it died immediately as he looked intensely displeased with her.

'Julia, you will appreciate that I have to make absolutely sure that if I let one of my students 'loose in Theatre', as you put it, that the patient will be in capable hands.'

'Yes, of course, I do appreciate that, but I've had a great deal of experience in Theatre and—'

'So I'm told,' he interrupted dryly. 'Your tutor in London, Don Grainger, gave you an extremely glowing reference, outlining some of the orthopaedic operations you have performed.'

She brightened up at this piece of news. What

a treasure Don Grainger had been during her medical-school days and after graduation.

'So,' Bernard continued in the same dour tone, 'during this illustrious career you're pursuing, how much experience have you had of hip replacements?'

Oh, joy! At last she was definitely on home ground! She began to elaborate at length on the hip replacements she'd undertaken, at first assisting before moving on to operating under supervision.

He interrupted to ask questions as she enthused about how she loved to remove the static, painful joint and replace it with a prosthesis. His questions concerned the types of prostheses she'd used, which she preferred and if she enjoyed following up the after-care of her patients.

'But of course I enjoy seeing my patients after I've spent so much time with them in Theatre. Seeing the patient before and after surgery, making sure they're getting the best possible after-care, is all part of the buzz a surgeon gets.'

'Buzz? What do you mean by this?'

In her enthusiasm for the subject she'd gone into English. Embarrassed at getting so carried away, she began to speak French again to dispel the wrinkles of concern that had appeared on his brow. 'It's the wonderful excitement of taking away pain and suffering and restoring a new, more active lifestyle to a patient. Not exactly what I meant but something like that.'

They were both silent for a few moments. The clock on the wall ticked away the seconds, reminding Bernard he had another student to see. He wished he didn't find this one so fascinating. Was it her enthusiasm for the subject or was it something he shouldn't even be thinking about every time he met up with her? She was his student, a career woman, and he was a family man. Never the twain should meet!

He put on his stern tutor expression as he stood up to indicate the interview was over.

'Send Dominic in, please.'

She turned and walked to the door, anxious to escape from the inquisition and the conflict of emotions she was experiencing.

'How was it?' Dominic asked as she came out.

She shrugged her shoulders. 'I've no idea how it went,' she whispered. 'Good luck!'

The next day she was still none the wiser. If anything, she was now feeling even more frustrated. She really was getting withdrawal symptoms from being just a cog in the machinery of this difficult course. She needed to actually make a major contribution to an interesting operation in Theatre, feel the buzz of satisfaction she was used to getting when an operation was a success and the patient's state of health vastly improved.

She looked up from the notes she'd been studying as Bernard walked in and took his place at the front of the tutorial room. The chattering between the students died down as ten pairs of eyes focussed on their professor. She thought he looked slightly worried this morning as he glanced around the room.

'Good morning.' A slight nod of the head in her direction as he acknowledged her, seated, as she had been so far this course, in the front row.

Bernard's serious expression didn't change as he began to explain what would happen that morning. They had admitted a patient three days before who had been on the waiting list for a hip replacement. Apparently, the lady in question was from a medical background herself. She had elected to have her operation under general anaesthetic and in the interests of furthering the education of the budding surgeons in Bernard's group she had agreed that her operation should be used for teaching purposes.

'Surgery begins at eleven this morning.' He seemed to be directing his statement right at her.

Why was he still looking at her? She tried to shrink down in her seat. He raised his eyes again to address the now apprehensive students.

'I shall be performing the operation with the help of a qualified and experienced junior surgeon and one of my students.'

He was looking at her again. She swallowed hard.

'I have deliberately given you no warning of this because there will be times in your future careers when you will be called upon to operate at short notice and I wanted to see how you handle the added adrenalin that sometimes causes panic amongst the less suitable candidates.'

He smiled. Thank goodness! It was as if the sun had come out. She shifted awkwardly in her seat, sensing that he was about to make an important announcement.

'The reason I sent out a questionnaire before you arrived here, asking about previous experience of hip replacement surgery, was to ascertain who might be a likely candidate for the first operation of the course. Several of you indicated varying degrees of competence. I consider that some of you would be perfectly capable of being my second assistant this morning.'

He read from a list, Julia holding her breath apprehensively after she heard her name read out.

'There's no need to be worried. We are a teaching hospital with excellent insurance.' His smile broadened. 'There is a stipulation that patients must be chosen with care and must agree to everything that might happen during their surgery. The patient we will operate on this morning is a retired surgeon herself and fully co-operative. Now…'

He paused and looked around the class. 'Who would like the opportunity to work with me this morning?'

Talk about adrenalin pumping! Her heart was pounding so quickly she felt everyone in the room would hear it. This was the opportunity she should seize on. The opportunity she'd asked Bernard for. The old Julia would have been leaping to her feet, desperate for the experience. These days she could feel real fear whenever opportunity knocked.

Seconds dragged by. Nobody had moved. Several throats had been cleared, including Bernard's. She could feel his eyes boring into her. What had her father always told her? Feel the fear and do it anyway.

Her hand shot up, seemingly having a life of its own. Every fibre of her body was warning her to hold off, not to stick her neck out, but this was why she'd come here. To challenge herself and banish her insecurities. She could do this! Raising her eyes tentatively towards the rostrum, she was rewarded by a look of intense pride.

Bernard knew he'd goaded her on that morning. He'd deliberately put her to the test and she hadn't failed him. He'd already seen for himself how knowledgeable she was about her passion but, from what he'd learned during their brief time since she arrived, she was a student who needed her confidence boosted. And this could only be done by subjecting her to difficult and demanding situations that required top-class skills, diligent training, impeccable qualifications and endless energy. The ability to carry on long after your whole body was experiencing real physical weariness, if required.

Though he didn't doubt that intellectually she was probably streets ahead of her louder colleagues he worried that she might not be physically strong enough at times. He would have the same concerns with any female student. A fact that had made him consider hard about offering her a place on this course. If he was honest with himself, he'd only admitted her to the course as a favour to his old friend Don Grainger. Don was no fool. He wouldn't have put her forward to take the course if he didn't think she was a natural surgeon.

But Julia still had to prove herself to him. Although he trusted his old friend, he needed to be in Theatre with her himself to actually make a sound judgement.

He composed his features back to the completely objective, professional tutor he was supposed to be. But it was difficult to hold back the elation he felt now that his plan had worked. The teacher in him wanted to build up her confidence, which he surmised had for some reason taken a knock somewhere along the way. The fact that he found her impossibly attractive must be dealt with as a separate issue, which couldn't in any way colour his professional judgement of her.

'Thank you, Julia. Would you meet me in the ante-theatre at ten-thirty, please? We shall be using the teaching theatre where those of you not required on the lower surgery area will sit on the raised seats behind the transparent screens. You will be able to hear everything, take notes and ask questions at the end of the operation.'

Julia dealt with the moment of panic that suddenly came over her. She needed to escape and scan her notes. She mustn't leave anything to chance during her debut in Theatre. And she wanted time to check out the patient. That was always important. She wasn't dealing with an abstract. This was a human being who deserved respect so perhaps it would be possible to...

Thoughts tumbled through her mind as she hurried to the door, only to find that Bernard was waiting there for her.

'Would you like to meet the patient?'

She gave a sigh of relief. 'That's definitely on my check list...along with everything else I need to do.'

'Don't worry. There's plenty of time.'

She revelled in his smooth, soothing voice and remembered that he must have had to go through difficult situations to reach the heights of his profession. She had a lot to prove to him so she felt intensely nervous because he still hadn't thawed out with her. Could she work alongside him without making a fool of herself?

She squared her shoulders. She would do the best for the patient, as she had always done, and Bernard's opinion of her didn't matter. Oh, but his opinion of you does matter, said a small, nagging voice in her head.

'You look nervous, Julia,' he said, as if reading her thoughts. 'Take a deep breath. Now let it out. That's better. I wouldn't let you operate on my patient if I didn't think you were capable, extremely capable according to your previous tutor.'

She felt as if she'd grown taller already and much stronger. Her thoughts were clearing and she could feel a list of priorities forming in her head.

He led her along the corridor, speaking now in a gentler tone than he usually used. She felt comforted, supported both physically and mentally.

His arm brushed hers as they walked together and she was surprised by the sparks of attraction his close proximity aroused. Not an easy situation to be in. Nervous of Bernard because he would be judging her performance in Theatre, concerned about their patient and surprised at the frequent frissons of attraction towards her boss. This was going to be an intensely difficult situation.

He had a difficult job as tutor to ten students who had begun to regard him as the enemy. But she was beginning to view Bernard differently. Again she felt a tingling down her spine and knew she mustn't give in to this strange insane feeling that was forcing itself upon her.

'You see, Julia, in most hospital situations the surgical team meet the patient before they operate, don't they? So I do like my students to be involved in the pre-operative and post-operative care of their patients, working alongside the full-time hospital staff.'

She felt her clinical interest rising along with the added interest engendered by simply being alongside this charismatic man. On this, her surgical debut day, when she wanted to use her skills and knowledge as best she could, she was also trying so hard not to let her personal interest in him get in the way.

'Yes, as I told you, I would very much like to meet our patient. You said she was a surgeon?'

'An extremely eminent surgeon here in France. As a student I was very much in awe of her.'

'So you've known her a long time?'

He smiled as he looked sideways at his demure companion, looking so fresh, so young, so infinitely…he checked his thoughts…capable. Yes, she was capable. That was all that mattered.

He composed his thoughts again. 'I feel we shall experience full co-operation from our learned colleague. She was a great help when I was a young student in Paris.'

They walked together along the corridor, he adapting his stride to her slower pace. In the orthopaedic ward Bernard led her into one of the single rooms.

'Hello, Brigitte. How are you this morning?'

The patient, who was seated in a comfortable armchair by the window, smiled and put down her newspaper.

'Bernard! I'm very well, thank you, and so relieved that I'm going to have my operation today.'

He introduced Julia as a well-qualified doctor from England who was working towards a career in orthopaedic surgery.

'Julia has had a great deal of surgical experience. She has been mentored by our esteemed colleague Don Grainger and comes to us with his own high recommendations.'

The patient smiled. 'High praise indeed from Don.'

'Well, he's been Julia's tutor since medical school and he wrote in glowing terms about her capabilities. So much so that I've decided to tell my designated assistant to remain on standby in the theatre. I may or may not need him. How would you both feel about that?'

Brigitte leaned forward towards Julia. 'I would be delighted to help you up the career ladder in any way I can, Julia. After the operation—at which, of course, you must assist—we must have a long chat. I truly miss my days in surgery but my arthritis cut my career short. I like to keep up with the latest developments, though.'

Bernard was waiting for Julia's answer. 'And how do you feel about assisting with the surgery, Julia?'

'Very honoured.' She felt confident. Why shouldn't she be, with such generous support from the patient and professor?

'Excellent!' Bernard smiled.

Jeanine, the orthopaedic sister, came in to explain that they were about to prepare their patient for surgery. Did Bernard wish to do a further examination? He said he would like a few minutes to show his assistant the extent of the arthritic damage to the hip. Brigitte, walking with a stick, made her way back to her bed and lay down with a thankful sigh of relief.

She pointed out the most painful areas of her leg, which were around the the head of the right femur. Bernard held up the X-rays so that Julia could see the extent of the arthritic erosion and they discussed the method they were going to use to remove the damaged bone and replace it with a prosthesis.

Leaving the patient to be prepared for Theatre by the nursing staff, Julia still felt slightly apprehensive but at the same time she realised how lucky she was to be given an ideal situation like this in which to move forward, gathering confidence along the way. At the same time she would not only be furthering her career, she would be easing the pain and improving the health of a patient, which was why she and all the members of her family had joined the medical profession.

She walked towards the medical quarters. She needed a few minutes of peace and quiet to gather her thoughts and focus on the operation in front of her. She no longer felt the need to check her notes. Every bit of knowledge she needed was stored in her brain. She'd assisted at a hip replacement before on several occasions, actually performing part of the surgery with an experienced surgeon hovering nearby, watching

her every move, ready to stop or correct anything he didn't approve of.

It wouldn't be any different this time, except
that it would be Bernard who would be doing
the hovering. And this affinity she felt with him,
this desperation to please him was something
that unnerved her. It wasn't just that he was her
chief in this situation. It was something more
than that. Something definitely emotional. An
emotional connection. And she was trying to
avoid emotion.

Where relationships were concerned she didn't
trust herself, judging by her track record. At
least she should leave all emotion outside the
door of the theatre and concentrate all her training and expertise on doing the best for her patient.

Bernard was waiting for her when she nervously
pushed open the swing doors of the ante-theatre.
He gave her a smile of encouragement.

'OK?'

She smiled back with a confidence she didn't

feel—yet! It would come back to her as soon as she started working. Concentrate on the patient, she told herself. Don't think about yourself. Remember the last time you assisted at a hip replacement. The outcome was excellent. The patient survived to live a useful life—and so did you!

She scrubbed up. A nurse helped her into her sterile gown.

'We're ready to begin, Bernard,' the anaesthetist said over the intercom.

They were ready. Julia was aware of the bright lights as she followed Bernard into the theatre. Indistinguishable faces appeared as blurs through the transparent screen. She made her way towards the motionless figure on the theatre table aware, not for the first time, that going into Theatre felt very much like going on stage.

She was so involved during the operation that she had no time to worry about herself. Her concentration was taken up completely by the task in hand. She found herself working harmoniously with Bernard. Sometimes he would nod to her across the shrouded figure on the table, indicating that she should perform the next stage while he supervised. All the procedures came back to her immediately as her fingers deftly performed what was required.

Time flew by and it seemed only minutes before she was finishing the final sutures. At that point she suddenly became aware of Bernard's eyes on her as they had been during the entire operation. She placed her final used instrument on the unsterile tray, which a theatre nurse was preparing to remove. As she did so she glanced up at Bernard's eagle eyes above his mask. She thought he was smiling but she couldn't be sure as he turned to speak to the theatre sister and began giving her instructions on the immediate after-care of their patient.

There was nothing more for her to do in Theatre. It was all over and she'd survived, and more importantly so had Brigitte. The patient was now being wheeled into the recovery room. As she made her way out through the swing doors, Bernard came up to speak to her.

'I think a debriefing session would be a good idea this evening, Julia.'

As he held open the swing door and followed her out, she allowed herself to admit that the sparks of attraction she'd felt as his gloved hand had brushed hers during the operation had been difficult to ignore. And when she'd looked up once to the eyes above the mask she'd had to take a deep breath to remain focussed and professional.

She looked up at him as they walked together along the corridor. 'Yes, that would be very helpful.'

'Come along to my office about six.'

He was pushing open the door of his office as he spoke as if anxious to be alone again. The door closed behind him and he walked across to his chair. He had to admit to himself that Julia really was a natural. Everything that Don had said about her was true. What Don had failed to mention about his prize student was how attractive she was.

What was it about Julia that made him feel

so physically moved when they were together? Even in Theatre, the place where usually he was at his most professional, he'd felt sparks of attraction. That time when he'd passed her an instrument and their gloved hands had briefly touched... He shouldn't be thinking like this!

He had a difficult ex-wife to deal with, a wonderful six-year-old son who should be his priority. He shouldn't even be allowing these insane thoughts to enter his mind. He leaned back in his chair and took a deep breath. That made it worse because he was sure he could still smell that subtle perfume that lingered around her.

Was he going mad? He switched on his computer and forced himself to begin writing up his notes on the operation.

Walking down the corridor, Julia had no idea what impression she'd given Bernard during the operation. He'd given her no indication of his assessment of her performance as he'd closed the door, seemingly anxious to get away from her.

Her confidence, which had been high in

Theatre, was now wavering but she reminded herself of the way he'd reassured her all the way through the operation. Now that she had time to reflect, she thought he'd even smiled into his mask on occasion and nodded approval as she'd used her initiative. And she was almost sure she'd heard him whisper, 'Well done!' as she'd finished the final suture—or had she imagined that?

But did it matter what Bernard thought of her performance? If she was satisfied that she'd given it one hundred per cent and made life easier for her patient then that was what really mattered, wasn't it? Seeking approbation from Bernard was not why she'd come here.

She walked away purposefully. She would make notes, be ready to ask questions and take the criticisms that would help make her a better surgeon in the future.

At six o'clock she was standing outside Bernard's office, waiting for the second hand to reach the top of her watch.

'Come in!'

He was sitting at his desk. He stood up and came towards her as she closed the door, motioning her to sit in one of the armchairs placed near the window. He took the other one and opened a file of notes. She put her briefcase on the floor at the side of her chair after taking out her own small laptop.

'So how do you think the operation went, Julia?'

She cleared her throat and launched into the questions she'd prepared, going through all the steps of the operation from the first incision to the final suture.

He answered all her questions carefully and lucidly while she made notes on her laptop.

She leaned back against the back of the armchair as he answered her final question, and looked across at him. The expression on his face gave nothing away for a few seconds until he relaxed and gave her a studied smile.

'Excellent! I like a student who has everything under control both during and after the operation. I've no doubt you'll make a first-class surgeon.'

She breathed a sigh of relief. She'd sensed his approval but until that moment she couldn't be sure she hadn't been imagining it.

She smiled back. 'Thank you, Bernard. So, do you have any questions for me?'

'Just one.' He hesitated. He really shouldn't say what was uppermost in his mind. But he planned to be very careful if he felt himself giving in to the wrong emotions.

'It's been a long and intense day. Your trip shouldn't all be about work, however. You are a visitor to France after all, so may I buy you a drink at the Maurice Chevalier?'

She hesitated for a couple of seconds. She doubted very much that Bernard had extended this invitation to any of her fellow students, but his offer had been very formal. She would be foolish to try and read too much into it. Finally she smiled and nodded her agreement.

As she closed her laptop and put it back in its

case she was aware of the now familiar tingling feeling running down her spine. Apprehension?

Yes, but it was something more than that, she admitted as she felt the light touch of Bernard's arm as he ushered her out through the door.

CHAPTER THREE

THE Maurice Chevalier was deserted when they first arrived. Julia breathed a sigh of relief. The last thing she wanted was to seen by her fellow students socialising with their tyrannical boss. She had mixed feelings about her motivation in accepting his offer to buy her a drink. Yes, he was thawing out towards her. But would her colleagues think this was favouritism? And should she be alone with him in a social situation given the insane feelings she'd been experiencing?

Very soon a trickle of sunset worshippers gradually filled up most of the tables overlooking the sea. She folded her white cashmere sweater on her lap as she sat down and breathed in the scent of the sea and this unspoiled stretch of the coast that she loved so much.

It was turning a bit chilly now that the sun

had disappeared behind a cloud so she would soon have an excuse to wear the new sweater that she'd fallen in love with when she'd been doing some last-minute panic buying in London . She didn't usually spend so much on clothes but she'd salved her conscience by convincing herself that anything that would boost her depleted confidence was a definite asset.

'What would you like to drink, Julia?'

'I'll have a Kir please, Bernard.'

He nodded before going inside to the bar, returning shortly with her crème de cassis and white wine aperitif and a pastis with ice and water for himself.

She smiled as he placed the drinks on the table. 'Thank you. I used to come here as a child with my parents and brothers when we were on holiday. My mother used to drink Kir. I knew it was a very grown-up drink but she allowed me a small sip. I loved the taste of the blackcurrant juice mixed in with white wine. As soon as I was old enough I tried one for myself and that became my favourite aperitif in the evenings.'

'To your grown-up Kir, Julia.' Bernard smiled as he raised his glass to her. He thought she looked so lovely now with the sun low in the sky on her face. What an enigma she was! To think that she had performed so self-assuredly in Theatre today and yet here she was reminiscing so naively about her childhood.

She smiled back as she took her first sip. 'Mmm! So reviving after a long day in hospital!'

'You deserve it after your performance this morning. I was proud of you—I mean, you're one of the students I selected from a large number of applicants who wanted a place on the course so it's good to know you didn't let me down.'

He hastily drank from his glass of pastis with ice, adding some water so that he wouldn't become too exuberant. He didn't want Julia to misinterpret his remarks. She might think he...well, he fancied her in some way. Perish the thought, he lied to himself, knowing full well that she was a most attractive woman and he'd better be careful or he might go overboard in his admiration.

But putting that aside, he told himself sharply, trying to leave his admiration out of the equation, whenever he discovered a talented student he found it very satisfying, euphoric almost! But he'd better hold back with the praise so that Julia would work hard throughout the course and not let him down. And he must also be aware that his delight in her achievements had to remain totally without emotional attachment.

Nevertheless, it was certainly true that he found himself drawn towards her in a way that a professor shouldn't think of his student. They were both adults, yes, but he mustn't let this attraction he felt affect his professional judgement of her during the months of hard work ahead.

He looked across the table. 'So tell me, Julia, what made you apply for this course?'

She hesitated before answering. 'Well…er… having survived a disastrous marriage that had been a total mistake, I felt it was time to make a fresh start and get on with my career. My family background also contributed to my decision. Mum and Dad, who'd planned to be surgeons when they were in medical school, had then taken a more practical route to become general practitioners because they fell in love, married when my eldest brother was on the way and...'

She broke off and took a deep breath. 'Sorry, Bernard, you don't need to know all this.'

'Oh, but I do. It's fascinating! Your story is similar to mine, in fact. I too come from a medical background where my parents gave up their ambitions in favour of family life. Please go on.'

She felt relieved she wasn't boring him. 'Well, as I told you before, GP parents and three brothers, now surgeons, meant I had to be a high achiever to get myself heard in the family. Fortunately I enjoyed studying my favourite subjects. Only when I hastily married Tony after a whirlwind courtship and found it so difficult to find the time for study did I question the sanity of becoming a surgeon.'

She leaned back against her chair, her eyes temporarily blinded by the sun low in the sky, setting behind the hillside that swooped down into the sea. She delved into her bag for her sunglasses.

'That's better.'

She paused to gather her thoughts. How much should she tell him? He was a good listener, seemed interested, but was he simply being polite?

'At times I despaired of my exhausting role of wife, stepmother, medical student…'

'So you hadn't qualified when you married. Why didn't you wait until…?'

'I thought I was madly in love! I'd never been in love before and the wonderful euphoric sensations I experienced when I first met Tony swept me along. For the first time in my life I entered a world that was quite different from my own.'

Bernard looked puzzled as he watched the vibrant expressions on her face. 'In what way was it different?'

'Tony was a very successful man, having made enormous profits in the building and property business, proud of the fact that he'd come from a deprived background and made something of himself. Money meant everything to him. He lived and breathed doing deals, buying expensive clothes for himself, for the children and for me. He told me he'd outgrown his first wife, she was lazy, an ex-model who'd let herself go and wouldn't keep up with his aspirations so he'd set her up in an expensive house where she could bring up their two children. He'd bought a luxurious flat in London where he could continue his wheeling and dealing.

'I found out later that his wife had divorced him because of his womanising, realising that she was happier without him. She'd been hoping for a huge divorce settlement but she was still waiting. Of course, I didn't know any of this when I first saw him at the opera.'

'The opera?'

She smiled. 'Oh, it was a business deal he was doing with a client and he clinched it by taking this man and his wife to a performance of *La Bohème*. Anyway, I'd gone along with a group of fellow medical students and we were queuing at the bar in the interval, trying to get a drink.

'Tony was in front of me and put on the charm when he gathered that we were all medical students. He insisted on buying everybody a drink before whisking me off to his table and introducing me to his business friends as a young doctor. With the benefit of hindsight I know I shouldn't have allowed myself to be swept away by an unknown man who liked to flash his cash but I was still young, impressionable, and having had a cloistered childhood this whirlwind from another exciting world seemed the epitome of sophistication.'

'But what about your own friends? Didn't they think…?'

'Oh, they were happy to accept the free drinks but they thought I'd gone mad…which actually I had, for the first time in my life! I'd always been so careful to toe the line and do everything my mother and father told me…especially my mother. She'd insisted I mustn't marry until I was well established in my career. She used to constantly tell me about how she'd sacrificed her ambitions and forced herself to be content with life as a country GP, married to a GP, struggling with a huge workload whilst bringing up a family.'

She looked across the table at Bernard, who was hanging on her every word. She took a deep breath as she remembered her totally out-of-character stupidity in those early days of her relationship with the charismatic but totally unreliable Tony.

'You see, I was totally blown away by Tony's charismatic aura. I'd never seen anyone like him before except on TV or in a film. Looking back and remembering, I can't believe how gullible I was in those days. I feel as if I'm remembering something that happened to someone else, a little sister if I'd had one, someone with no experience of real life—which, in a way, was exactly how I was. I couldn't take my eyes off this tall, handsome character in the well-cut, expensive suit who seemed to demand attention from everybody who was listening to his deep, sexy voice.'

She paused as the weird memories from her past came back to her.

She took a deep breath as she watched Bernard's reaction. Yes, he was a good listener and definitely seemed to want her to continue.

'Tony was proud of the fact that he was a self-made man who'd come from a poor background. At the time I just couldn't help admiring him and then the admiration blossomed into something more dangerous and I fell for him, hook, line and sinker, whilst enjoying the fact that he seemed attracted to me.'

'So he was impressed by the fact that you were a medical student?'

'Oh, he thought I was a good catch. He told me during our disastrous marriage that he'd thought I must be from a wealthy family because we were all doctors. How wrong he was! Our education was the top priority to my parents and that made a big hole in the family budget.

'What I didn't realise was that his business deals were getting fewer and further between and he needed to find a wealthy wife to help keep him in the lifestyle he'd got used to during his successful years. My parents met him for the first time at our registry office wedding. My mother could hardly disguise her dislike of him and she made no secret of the fact that I'd let her down badly. That hurt…that really hurt.'

Her voice faltered as she remembered the angst she'd suffered, knowing full well that it was all her fault, knowing she'd hurt her mother who'd given up so much to raise her family. She shifted in her seat, pulling the sweater around her shoulders as she glanced away from Bernard towards the beautiful seascape in front of them. Maybe she should stop talking about her past and give him a chance to recover from his busy day.

'Bernard, you're a good listener but I don't want to bore you.'

'Please continue! I'm fascinated. I can see where you're coming from now. I do like to take an interest in the background of my students. As you say in England, it helps if I know what makes them tick, isn't it, Julia?'

'Yes, you got that exactly right, Bernard. You're finding out what makes me tick.'

He leaned across the table. 'I can tell you already, having known you only a couple of days. You're aiming for the top and it isn't easy, believe me. You'll reach the next peak and what will you find? Another peak to climb!'

He broke off. 'Please do go on. So you married this man from a different world? Were you happy at first?'

'Well, for the first few weeks of our marriage Tony boasted to all his associates—I won't call them friends because they were mostly hangers-on intent on helping themselves to his dwindling cash—about his clever young wife who was going to be a doctor. But the problem was that he thought I could pass my exams without spending time studying, be the perfect stepmother to his children when they came to stay at weekends, be a good hostess to his clients—and I quickly realised it wasn't possible. That's when it all turned nasty. His attitude completely changed. He seemed to think that by shouting at me he could turn me into superwoman, perfect in everything he wanted me to do for him.'

'You have another saying in England—marry

in haste, repent at leisure. Isn't that right?' Bernard was watching her reaction. 'Was that what happened?'

'Exactly! He changed completely once the ring was on my finger and he realised my family hadn't endowed me with money. One of the things he told me before we married was that having fathered twins who were then five, a boy and a girl, he didn't want any more children. It was a struggle to come to terms with that because I'd always hoped I would have children of my own when I'd established my career.

'I subjugated my own desires for parenthood by immersing myself in taking care of my stepchildren. I loved those two as if they were my own and it was a terrible wrench when we split up and I lost all contact with them.'

Bernard noticed the emotional waver in her voice as she said this. Yes, he could see she would adore starting a family. Warning bells were ringing in his head. He mustn't get too familiar with her.

'So what caused you to split up?'

'It was pressures of my work and trying to take care of my stepchildren. Tony, not being from a medical background, just didn't understand. I adored the children, bonded with them and began to put them before my medical studies, but Tony was still dissatisfied with the amount of time I could spare him. He began to look elsewhere.

'Everything came to a head one fateful weekend just six months after we were married. I was trying to get to grips with some revision in the study and was working on my computer when he flung open the door and told me to leave all that medical stuff and get into some expensive clothes. It was important that I should get out of my scruffy tracksuit and tart myself up so that I looked drop-dead gorgeous. He'd been speaking to a prospective client and he was taking him and his wife out for lunch. The wife, apparently, was a real doll and knew how to dress so I'd better make the effort.'

She took another deep breath as the awful memories of that occasion came flooding back.

'I pointed out that I had an exam on the Monday and I needed to study...'

She broke off as she remembered how miserable she'd felt. Bernard put his hand across the table and laid it over her slender fingers. 'Julia, you don't have to tell me if it's too awful to remember.'

She swallowed hard. The touch of his fingers and his obvious concern for her unnerved her. Careful! Be very careful. Don't mistake sympathy with emotional involvement.

'Tony told me he was fed up with seeing me studying. I was no fun any more. And then he blurted out that he'd met somebody else. He wanted a divorce.'

'So...what did you do?'

'To be honest, I'd had enough and it was a blessed relief to think that I could walk away from the hell that my life had become. I asked him to have my things sent to the medical school. He said he would make all the necessary arrangements for my stuff to be sent wherever I wanted. I took my laptop and a few books, went back to the medical school and tried to concentrate on the exams looming after that disastrous weekend.'

'You must have felt…'

'I felt relieved to escape from Tony.' She shivered at the bad memories that still haunted her, often preventing her from sleeping in the night. 'But terribly sad to lose contact with the children.'

They sat for a few moments in silence. Bernard had been deeply moved by the story of her marriage. He could see how she would need her confidence to be boosted at every possible moment. But he mustn't go overboard. Mustn't allow emotion to take over. Yet he didn't want to cut short the evening and they both needed a meal after their long day.

'Let's go inside and have something to eat. That's if you'd like to,' he added. 'Maybe you've got other plans tonight, meeting up with friends from the group or…'

'No plans tonight except to relax.' She smiled

up at him. He was already standing, looking down at her.

He led the way. Inside, the warmth of the sun had made the place feel cosy and inviting. He held out her chair for her. The waiter came along and Bernard asked what the *plat du jour* was.

'Always best to get the main dish that's been cooked that day in these small places, don't you think?'

She felt very comfortable with him as he ordered the coq au vin for them. It came in a large casserole dish. Bernard dug the large serving spoon into the centre and helped her to a generous portion.

'Hey, steady on!' she said, reaching across to touch his wrist. A shiver went down her spine, a quite different shiver to the cold one she'd experienced outside. She felt they must have met somewhere before in a former life. She put both hands back in her lap.

'Did you live near here when you were a child, Bernard?'

He passed her plate across to her. 'I was born

just five miles from here, up there in the valley beyond the hills. My grandparents were farmers. The farm is still there, but my father decided he wanted to be a doctor. He went off to medical school in Paris—like I did—and after qualifying he did a course in general practice so that he could come back to our village and fill a very real need. He set up practice in a room at the end of the house and my mother acted as receptionist and nurse besides running the family. She had trained as a nurse in Boulogne but she was born in the village.'

She swallowed a spoonful of the delicious chicken casserole. 'Did you have brothers and sisters?'

He shook his head sadly. 'No, my mother wanted to have more children but it didn't happen. She died of ovarian cancer when I was six.'

'That must have been awful for you and your father. However did you cope?'

'My father employed a lady from the village to help out as nurse, receptionist and housekeeper but it was hard for him to adapt. He also employed her daughter Marianne to help her mother with the housekeeping and look after me. She's still working up there at the farm just as she did when she was sixteen. She took care of me from the time I was six and when she married in her late teens her husband moved in to work on the farm. They became part of the family.'

He hesitated for a moment as if to compose himself. 'I was fifteen when my father died. He'd never been the same since my mother's death. He went through the motions of being a competent doctor but one harsh winter he succumbed to a bout of influenza that turned to pneumonia. I think he simply lost the will to live without my mother.'

They were both silent for a while, engrossed in their own thoughts as the delicious, home-cooked food revived them.

Bernard cleared his throat and put down his spoon. 'I always wanted to marry someone who would be my soul mate as my parents had been together,' he said huskily. 'But it didn't happen.

Like you, I was mistaken about the partner I chose—or did she choose me?'

He gave her a whimsical smile. 'If only I could turn the clock back. Apart from the fact that I wouldn't have had my wonderful son, Philippe, if I hadn't met Gabrielle.'

She leaned back in her chair, watching the sad expression that flitted across his face. The young families around them were departing now, mothers ushering their offspring out of the door as fathers paid the bills. It was all so nostalgic. Why couldn't she have replicated something like this? Why couldn't Bernard?

It wasn't just that both of them were career minded, both aiming to climb the peaks to the top of their chosen profession. It was possible to have a career and a family—but not yet! The timing was wrong. She mustn't get ideas about the rapport building up between them. She mustn't fantasise about developing a meaningful relationship with Bernard.

'How often do you see your son?'

'As often as I can escape from my work. I'm

going to Paris this weekend to see him. Philippe lives with Gabrielle in her mother's house, which is very convenient. His grandmother dotes on him and has been a tower of strength to all of us when my wife was…well, lacking in maternal instinct and hell bent on—'

He broke off. 'No, you don't want to hear all the sordid details of our less than perfect marriage.'

She wanted to say, Oh yes, I do. She liked to hear about other people making mistakes in their lives. It made her feel in some way that she wasn't the only naive idiot where relationships were concerned. But she remained silent

'I'll get the bill.' He signalled for the waiter. Suddenly he was turning back into the professional as his thoughts turned to the work ahead.

'I've asked Dominic to assist me tomorrow in Theatre. He came to me this afternoon and said he would be happy to assist. It just so happens I've got to do a knee replacement tomorrow morning so I'll be able to put him through his paces. He's had a lot of experience but wasn't brave enough to volunteer for the first opera-tion of the class.' He stood up and moved round to hold the back of her chair. As they walked to the door he said, 'Thank you for setting the ball rolling today, Julia. You'll be a difficult act to follow.'

As they walked back together towards the hospital she was aware of his hand hanging loosely by his side. She so wished he would take hold of hers but she realised he was in professional mode again. Just as well when she'd decided to keep a rein on her own emotions.

'I've got to do some work,' he said briskly, not trusting himself to relax his guard as they stood together outside the main door of the hospital. He did have work to do in his consulting room but he was trying to ignore his real feelings. What he wanted to do was whisk her back to his rooms in the medics' quarters and… No, don't go there, he told himself as he looked down at her beautiful face turned up towards his.

'So have I,' she said quickly, knowing full well that all she wanted to do was have a hot shower and climb into bed. The shower should help to take away the mad emotions running through her mind and her body, but would she be able to sleep?

'Goodnight, Julia. See you tomorrow.'

He bent down and brushed the side of her face with his lips, telling himself they were off duty now and hospital protocol had no place in this private moment. He mustn't give anyone cause to think that he was favouring one of his students because he wasn't. But he couldn't bear to let her go without some brief contact. Anyway, it was normal to exchange kisses on the cheek in France after spending the evening with a pleasant companion.

She walked quickly in the opposite direction from his consulting room, taking the long way round to her study-bedroom in the medics' quarters. She didn't look back.

He watched the slight, slim figure in the beautiful white sweater and figure-hugging black trousers turning the corner at the end of the corridor. He'd better wait a few moments before he made his way to his own study-bedroom, where he planned to sleep that night. He felt too tired to drive out to the farm and he'd had a couple of glasses of wine with the meal. He could go and do some work in his consulting rooms but he didn't think it would be easy to concentrate tonight.

He realised the nurse on Reception was watching him. He hoped he'd given Julia enough time to disappear into her room.

He let the water cascade over him as he soaped himself with shower gel. His mind was buzzing with conflicting ideas. It was going to be so difficult to keep his growing admiration for Julia under control. He had to remain totally professional. But that was easier said than done.

He stepped out of the shower and reached for a towel. He'd hoped the hot water would help to put him in a steadier mood. It had been a long time since he'd felt like this. As he dried himself and threw the towel towards the laundry bin he recognised the symptoms only too well. It wasn't necessary to have medical qualifications to recognise that he was very attracted to Julia. And he wanted to go along with this mad, wonderful feeling. But it could be disastrous!

He climbed between the cool sheets, kicking at the corners where the maid had tucked them in. That was better. One of the perks of being a consultant was that you had daily maid service and a decent-sized room. He thought of the tiny room where Julia would be cloistered and hoped she was comfortable. She would have forgotten all about him and knowing how conscientious she was she would be reading up about knee-replacement operations.

He put his hands behind his head and leaned back against the pillow as he thought about how she had suffered with her marriage. He would have liked to talk about his own marriage with her but had decided against it even though he just knew she would have lent him a sympathetic ear. But he'd never told anyone the full story of what had gone wrong with Gabrielle. He'd been every bit as gullible as Julia! But at least he had his adorable son, Philippe, to dote on—the one good thing to have come from that ill-advised union.

Which reminded him about the latest bomb-shell his ex-wife had dropped recently. She was planning to get married again. The prospective husband was rich apparently but also consider-ably older than she was with grown-up children from a previous marriage and he didn't want a young child around the house. So she'd asked him to have Philippe live with him.

Bernard knew he would be absolutely thrilled at having Philippe with him. He'd already planned ahead so that the new arrangement would work. Philippe could stay at the farm dur-ing the day with Marianne, go to the local school as he'd done, make friends in the village. He felt the excitement rising at the prospect. But it was tinged with apprehension about how Veronique, Gabrielle's mother, would react.

His ex-wife hadn't yet told her mother of her plans. It would be too cruel to simply take Philippe away. He was like her own son and she'd poured all her considerable maternal love into his upbringing to the age of six. He would have to make sure Veronique came over to see Philippe and that he took his son to Paris as often as he could.

He could feel the doubts creeping in already and knew that if he was really honest with himself the situation was far from solved. Ah, well, he'd have to contend with that problem this weekend when he went to Paris. Meanwhile, he'd better try to get some sleep.

He allowed himself to think about Julia as he closed his eyes, alarmed at the physical reaction surging through his body. If only he'd been able to bring her back here, make love to her and then fall asleep with her in his arms.

He knew that it was going to take an effort on his part but he had to stop thinking like this, definitely try to see her only in a professional situation. Yes, that was what he should do. But whether he could keep to this resolution was a different matter.

CHAPTER FOUR

As JULIA showered in the tiny bathroom tucked away in the corner of her study-bedroom her thoughts turned to the day ahead. Hard to believe she'd been here more than a month. The last five weeks had flown by so quickly as she'd tried hard to put all her energy into adapting to her new situation.

She stepped out of the shower and grabbed a large fluffy towel. A whole weekend stretched ahead of her. Two whole days when she was going to try and catch up on her sleep, do some work on the notes she'd taken during Bernard's tutorials and then spend some time outside in the glorious June sunshine.

For the past few weeks she'd spent far too much time indoors, in Theatre and in the wards, seeing the pre-operative and post-operative patients in her care. On two occasions she'd been called in to help out in the *Urgences* department, the French equivalent of Accident and Emergency. She'd enjoyed all her work, giving all her energies and expertise to the patients and ensuring she learned and made notes on every important medical experience to store up for future reference.

But as she pulled on her jeans and a favourite old black T-shirt she knew she'd neglected her own health and strength in her desire to embrace every situation in her new life. It was something her parents had constantly chided her about. But it had been a case of 'Do as I say, not do as I do.' She'd long ago realised she was inherently disposed to using up her energy and then falling back on her frazzled nerves with an empty tank of petrol—just like her parents and brothers.

Nevertheless, she had work to do this morning before she could play. She sat down at her desk and reached for her laptop and the notebook that was always in her bag. She tried to put as much information straight onto the laptop but in many situations where she had a hands-on approach this was impossible.

She particularly enjoyed Bernard's tutorials because they seemed to be the only times she saw him nowadays—when they were in a professional situation. He'd definitely thawed out with all of his students and she'd noticed he'd gained their respect now that they appreciated how much he wanted them all to succeed.

She'd been particularly amazed—and gratified!—when he'd praised her in front of all the students, saying she'd made him reassess his opinion of female orthopaedic surgeons. 'I've no doubt now that Julia is inherently talented and a natural at this type of surgery.'

She'd been delighted by his praise, but slightly apprehensive. She worried that her fellow students would tease her for being teacher's pet. She needn't have worried on that score because they crowded aound her at the end of the tutorial, congratulating her. Those who'd watched her debut performance were especially complimentary.

Dominic had actually kissed her on both cheeks, and as she glanced at their tutor on the rostrum she'd seen him frowning with disapproval. Strange. She didn't know what to make of that. Dominic was ever the flamboyant one of the crowd and she'd made a point of discouraging any advances. While she enjoyed spending time in Dominic's company, if she was honest with herself it was Bernard's attentions she longed for.

She wondered what he was doing this weekend. She knew he'd been off to Paris to see his son on the weekend after they'd enjoyed supper together at the Maurice Chevalier. She'd looked forward to his return but on the Monday morning, as they'd worked together, he'd seemed distant, preoccupied even. During a coffee break, when all her colleagues had been with them, she'd plucked up courage, hoping to break the ice, and asked him if he'd enjoyed his weekend. He'd answered briefly that, yes, it had made a change from hospital life.

From the pained expression on his face she'd

deduced it hadn't been a total success. But there had been something else in his manner towards her. Without being overtly cold, he was putting her at arm's length, as it were. Making it obvious that perhaps he regretted being so warm towards her after her debut performance in Theatre. At least, that was how she'd taken it. So she'd thrown herself into her work and reined in her emotions, which, yes, she admitted it now, had been getting out of control.

But it hadn't been easy. She was still plagued by embarrassing thoughts about him. Thoughts that had nothing to do with real life and never could become reality...could they? She was like a teenager with a crush on the teacher! She should get out more, which she was definitely going to do this morning after she'd done some work on her notes.She sighed as she opened up and began reading the scribbled notes, remembering how she'd hung on every word as Bernard had delivered an off-the-cuff mini-lecture about performing amputations a couple of days ago. The importance of preparing the patient both physically and mentally. And then the after-care, the importance of listening, referring the patient to the best professional care. She'd been totally enthralled by his sympathetic approach, by the stories he'd told them about his secondment as an army surgeon in a war zone overseas. Some of his descriptions of what that had entailed had brought tears to her eyes because she'd found herself thinking she was so glad that he hadn't had to have a limb amputated.

That beautiful body of his—well, she assumed it was magnificent beneath the well-cut suits. Occasionally when he took off his jacket and rolled up his sleeves in a practical situation she'd seen muscles that looked as if they should be on one of those statues she'd seen when she'd wandered around the Louvre in Paris.

She made a determined effort to gather her thoughts and get back to the real work in hand.

A couple of hours later she got up from her desk and pulled on her jeans and a T-shirt. Scraping her long blonde hair into a ponytail, she hurried out of her room, anxious to get on the beach before it got too hot.

In a room not too far away down the corridor that was reserved for senior staff Bernard was also working on his laptop. He was transcribing notes for a paper he had to deliver at a conference in Paris soon. He'd been putting it off as he'd had to spend a lot of time with his students during the last month. They were an intelligent group and the work was enjoyable but time consuming.

He glanced at his watch. Good thing he'd started early that morning. He'd still have to finish off the paper while Philippe was here. He'd promised to take him to the beach. Perhaps if he took him there this morning they could go up to the farm, have lunch and then he could work for a couple of hours while Marianne took care of Philippe.

He phoned the farm. Marianne was delighted with the arrangement he proposed. 'Yes, take Philippe to the beach for the good sea air before you come out here for lunch. Your rooms are ready, of course. See you soon, Bernard!'

He started to get ready for the arrival of his son. Philippe's car, driven by the uniformed chauffeur, would arrive soon from Paris. This was one of the perks that Gabrielle had got used to since she'd begun dating the wealthy Frederic—her soon-to-be husband.

Julia walked briskly down to the beach. As the warm summer breeze fanned her cheeks she felt reinvigorated. This was exactly what she needed today. Fresh air. No work. No worries!

She skipped down the wooden steps that led onto the sand and broke into a gentle jog. As her breathing improved to a steady rhythm she increased her pace to a gentle run. Mmm, it was good to know her limbs hadn't seized up as she worked endlessly in hospital! She ran towards the sea and began to follow the shoreline.

'Julia?'

She turned at the sound of a man's voice. A little way up the beach a man in a T-shirt and shorts was digging a moat round a sandcastle. A child was helping him.

'Bernard?' She stood still, panting to get her breath back.

Bernard stopped digging and leaned on his spade. 'I don't mean to disturb your run but I'd love you to meet my son.'

She smiled as she walked up the beach towards him. He came towards her. Her heart, which had increased its rate due to her running, was now beating even more rapidly.

The young boy followed behind.

'Hello.' She smiled down at the young boy who turned to his father, looking up at him adoringly whilst waiting to be enlightened as to who the lady was.

'This is Julia, Philippe.'

Philippe extended his hand towards her. 'Hello, *mademoiselle.*'

She gave the charming boy a big smile. 'Oh, please call me Julia,' she said in French. 'Have you come from Paris this morning?'

Bernard watched her easy rapport with his

son. It gave him a warm feeling but warning bells rang. Julia was only here for six months. He mustn't allow a rapport to build up between them. Philippe would be sad when she had to leave. So would he!

'Yes, I came by car. Are you a doctor here, like Papa?'

'Yes, I'm a doctor but I'm also a student on the course that your father is in charge of. I'm learning how to improve my surgical skills.'

'Oh, yes, Papa has told me all about it. I'm going to be a surgeon when I grow up.'

'Are you?'

'Papa tells me I'll have to work very hard if I want to be a surgeon. Papa works hard all the time. Look at the castle he's building for me, Julia.'

'It's beautiful! A real work of art.'

'What's a work of art?'

'Well, it's something that's beautiful.'

'I've been digging the moat round it and piling the sand on the castle while Papa made the work-of-art bit at the top. I'm going to run down to the sea now and bring back some water in my bucket.'

Julia smiled down at the eager young boy. 'If you start digging a channel down to the sea, the incoming tide will flow into it and come all the way up to the moat round your castle.'

Wide eyes stared up at her in amazement. 'Will it really, Julia? Will you help me?'

She'd been totally unaware that Bernard had been watching with mixed emotions the two of them getting on so well together. He could feel the poignancy of the encounter and the feelings he was experiencing were difficult to understand.

She glanced across at him, her maternal instincts making her want to spend time with this adorable child but at the same time wondering how Bernard would feel. To her relief he was smiling fondly at the pair of them.

'That's a brilliant idea, Julia. Are you sure you can spare the time? I know your tutor has a reputation for pushing you hard!'

She smiled back at him. 'I'm giving myself

the whole day off to recharge my batteries.' She turned back to the little boy, who was still waiting for her answer. 'I'd love to help you, Philippe. Have you got a spare spade?'

Bernard picked up a large plastic bag and passed her a spare spade.

'Thank you.'

His hand, covered in sand, felt rough as it touched hers. She looked up at him and her heart seemed to stand still. She allowed herself to look into his eyes for a second longer before she turned back to his son.

'Come on, Philippe. Let's show Papa how hard we can work together.'

Bernard leaned against his spade as he watched Julia take his son to the edge of the sea. As they sprinted together she looked so young. Her long blonde hair had escaped the band she'd tied round it and was flowing over her shoulders. He couldn't help thinking how much more attractive she looked now than when she had to imprison it in a theatre cap. And, heaven knew, she had a serious effect on him in Theatre even without that tantalising hair showing!

He shouldn't be thinking like this. How many times had he reprimanded himself for breaking his self-made rule of no commitment ever again? And before his eyes he could see the rapport developing between Julia and Philippe.

They were digging their channel now. The tide was coming in and beginning to trickle into it. Throwing aside all his reservations about relationships, he ran down the beach to join them. This was what he needed. Some carefree relaxation. If Julia could give herself a day off, so could he.

The channel grew much quicker now with three of them working together. In no time at all it had reached the moat of the castle and water was trickling in, slowly at first and then more quickly.

Bernard put the finishing touches to the crenellated edge at the top of the castle before reaching into the bag for a small boat.

'Here you are, Philippe. See if your boat will sail round the castle now.'

'Oh, it's brilliant! Look at my boat, Papa!' The little boy was clapping his hands with delight, stopping occasionally to push the boat if it got stuck in the side of the castle. 'Round and round and round and…'

'That was a brainwave of yours, Julia,' Bernard said quietly. 'I can see you've done this a few times.'

She smiled. 'I have indeed. And on this very beach. But the tide's coming in very quickly now so Philippe had better make the most of it. Not long before you'll have to pack up and leave. I'll help gather up your things.'

Together they gathered up the plastic beach toys and Bernard stuffed them back into the large bag. A particularly strong surge of water flooded the moat and he called out to Philippe that they would have to go now.

'No, Papa, I don't want to go!'

Another surge of water swirled around Philippe's ankles. 'OK! I'm coming.'

Philippe ran to his father for safety, putting his arms around his legs. Bernard hoisted him up onto his shoulders and picked up the bag then they all hurried up the beach.

'I've got my car parked on the promenade. I'm taking Philippe up to my farm. Julia, can I give you a lift back to hospital or are you going to keep running on the path up there now that the tide will soon be in? Alternatively...'

He hesitated only a second before putting to her the idea that had been forming in his mind.

'Would you like to come up to the farm with us as you've given yourself a day off from the tyranny of your endless work schedule?'

'Oh, Julia, please say you'll come! I can show you the sheep and the cows and the—'

'That sounds really exciting, Philippe.' She shouldn't accept this invitation but she desperately wanted to. She salved her conscience by telling herself that it would be good for Philippe to have someone other than his father to amuse him. 'Thank you, Bernard, I'd love to see your farm.'

'Hurrah!'

Bernard had already justified his invitation by telling himself that Julia obviously loved children and might like to amuse Philippe while he got on with some work that afternoon. He led the way up the steps and along the promenade to the car.

Philippe had slipped his little hand inside Julia's and was chatting happily to her about the farm, the animals and all the other delights of the place that was his home when he was with his beloved Papa.

'You don't mind sitting in the back, I hope? Philippe is happier there if he's got someone to talk to and you both seem to have a lot to discuss.'

'Oh, we've got a lot to talk about, haven't we, Philippe? So, did you drive yourself over from Paris this morning?'

Philippe giggled. 'I'm only six.'

'Oh, I thought you were much older.'

'Philippe is six going on sixteen, actually.'

She smiled, positively glowing at the attentions

of father and son. Bernard was leaning through the door of the car, checking on Philippe's seat belt and pointing out hers. He was very close as he leaned across to check on both of them. As he straightened up and prepared to close the car door their eyes met and Julia felt a frisson of pure excitement mingled with apprehension running through her. She felt emotionally warm and cosseted and decided to simply go with the flow for a few hours. No point worrying too much about where all this might be leading

There was absolutely nothing wrong with them being friends, she decided. But as she looked up at the expression on Bernard's face she held her breath.

His expression was one of total admiration as he looked at her and she could feel her confidence zooming higher. Bernard was so good for her professional confidence. She remembered how he'd praised her in front of her colleagues. That had given her ego a much-needed boost after the knocks she'd taken in the past. This was what she needed, a totally platonic friendship. The fact that she was only here for just over four more months and shouldn't be building a rapport with Bernard's son was still at the back of mind, but for today she shelved the problem. A day off was a day off from worry.

Bernard drove them out onto the main road.

'I'm going to drive as soon as I'm old enough, Julia. Thomas was explaining about his car this morning when we came down this hill. It's such a clever car, it changes gears all by itself. Papa has to change his own gears in this car, don't you?'

'It makes me feel more in control.' Bernard shifted down a gear as the hill grew steeper.

'Thomas says he'll teach me to drive when I'm older.'

Bernard remained quiet. Who knew what the future held? There were so many hurdles to negotiate in the new situation that his ex-wife had thrust upon them.

Julia was also confused about the man Thomas but she didn't want to ask questions. It was Philippe who provided a clue.

'Thomas took his cap off when we got outside Paris. Mummy likes him to wear it when he takes us shopping. He's Frederic's chauffeur.' He leaned towards Julia. 'I think Mummy is going to marry him soon—well, she keeps telling me she is. I hope we don't have to move into his house. It's so quiet and Frederic won't let me use his computer. I was only looking at it one day when he came in and he got really cross with me. I wasn't going to play games on it or anything like that.'

Bernard pulled into a parking area saying that this was a good place to admire the view. There was a tight feeling in his chest. The revelations that his son made every time he saw him made his heart bleed. The sooner he finalised the custody preparations and got Philippe over here, the better. He got out of the car and opened the back doors.

'Wonderful view, isn't it?'

Julia heard the emotion in his voice and saw the sad expression in his eyes. She could only guess at the situation that had developed in

Bernard's life and he was obviously deeply concerned about his son's welfare.

Bernard was taking hold of Philippe's hand as he jumped out onto the grass. 'Keep hold of my hand, Philippe. I don't want you to roll down the hillside and end up in the sea.'

Philippe giggled. 'That would be fun!'

'Do you know, Philippe, I used to stand here admiring the view with my *papa* and mummy when I was younger?' Julia said.

'Really! Papa told me that you live in England.'

'Oh, I do live in England but we used to spend our holidays in France. My mother is French and my father is English. My mother was keen we should speak French all the time when we were in France so we would enlarge our French vocabulary.'

She broke off as she noticed the puzzled expression on the young boy's face. 'Sorry, Philippe, I keep forgetting you're only six. What I'm trying to say is that we needed as much practice as we could get to make sure we spoke good

French. My grandmother lived over those hills there in Montreuil sur Mer.'

She pointed her finger towards the hills they'd travelled over so often.

'We used to stay with her when I was small and after she died we continued coming over to France and staying here on the coast for our holidays.'

Bernard was smiling across at her appraisingly.

She smiled back. He looked like a man who was also taking a day off from his worries.

'Philippe is so intelligent I'm speaking to him as if he were much older,' she said quietly.

'I entirely approve. I do the same myself. Expand his knowledge as much as you can if he's interested. If he gets bored he'll switch off. It's a fascinating world if he's with the right people while he's growing up.'

Philippe was anxious to be included in the conversation again. 'So, Julia, when did you learn to speak French properly like you do now?'

She thought hard. 'I sort of learned it alongside learning to speak English—as a child. It seemed natural to speak English to my father and French to my mother. My brothers learned in the same way.'

'How many brothers have you got?'

'Three brothers, all older than me.'

'They must be very old. Are they as old as Papa?'

'My eldest brother, John, is about the same age as your father, I think. One time when we were standing here John started walking down that steep slope when my parents weren't looking. His trainers slipped on the wet grass and he tumbled a long way down the field until he managed to stop.'

'Was he hurt?'

'No, but his clothes were all grass stained and muddy. My mother wasn't too pleased.'

Philippe giggled. 'It must be fun, having brothers to play with. Frederic, Maman's fiancé, has got a few grown-up children but I don't think he likes them very much. They don't come to see him. He's very old, you see, and he gets tired.'

Julia looked across at Bernard. As their eyes met she could see his desolate expression deepen. Poor Bernard! She wanted to lean across the top of Philippe's head and give him a big hug—in a totally platonic, friendly way, of course. She mustn't lose sight of the fact that she'd come out to France for a fresh start and here she was becoming involved with another ready-made family, just as she had with Tony.

But Bernard wasn't like Tony. Nobody could be as bad as Tony. But what did she know about men? Only that if they wanted you they were charming and attentive at first. When they were fed up with you they moved on to someone else.

'Come on, let's all get back in the car. There's a storm brewing up over the sea.' Bernard was pointing out towards the horizon. 'Can you see the white flecks on the top of the waves, Philippe?'

'Yes, it's so exciting. The white flecks on the waves look like white horses riding over the waves. Oh, look up there, Papa! The sky's getting all dark. Where's the sun gone? Can't we wait here till it really arrives, Papa?'

'It's better to get to the farm so we don't get wet.'

Bernard drove over the brow of the steep hill and started down the other side. The road was narrow with tortuous bends. He drove carefully because the rain was now pelting down and hail-stones were bouncing on the slippery road.

'I remember coming over into this valley as a child and seeing that village down there! Difficult to see it in all this rain but I know it's there.'

Bernard switched on the car lights, hoping that if another vehicle drove towards him it would also have its lights on.

'We can't see the farm in this bad weather but we'll soon be there. It's on the other side of the village.'

It was a difficult but short drive down the hill. The rain began to ease off as they drove through the village. Bernard pointed out various landmarks—the village school, the *tabac*, the *alimentation*, which sold groceries.

'There's no *boulangerie* these days. A van comes over from the next village and delivers the bread to the *dépôt de pain*—that building over there, which doubles as the newsagent.'

They were soon driving out of the village towards the farm. The gate was open. Smoke was curling from a chimney.

'Strange to see smoke from a chimney in June,' Julia said.

'We have an ancient wood stove in the kitchen, which is never allowed to go out.'

'I help Marianne put wood on the stove when I come to stay with Papa. Look, there she is.'

A plump, middle-aged lady was coming towards the car, carrying a large umbrella.

Bernard got out and took charge of the umbrella. 'Philippe, you go into the house with Marianne. I'll bring Julia under the umbrella I've got in the boot of the car.'

She felt a firm arm going around her waist as she moved towards the kitchen door. They were sheltered from the rain by the umbrella but as she splashed through the puddles she glanced down at her mud-splashed workout clothes.

'Oh, dear,' said Bernard. 'Looks like your clothes have taken a bit of a beating.'

Julia laughed. 'Are you trying to say I look a mess?'

His grip tightened around her waist as he steadied her advance towards the kitchen door. Rain was dripping from the edge of the umbrella all around them but for a brief moment she felt as if they were the only people in the world. He'd pulled her to a halt and was looking down at her with such a strange expression on his handsome face. She felt her heart beating madly.

She knew this was another of those magic moments in life that she would never ever forget. For a brief moment she allowed herself to think that nothing else mattered except this magic feeling that was running through her.

'Papa, hurry up!'

'We're coming, Philippe.'

CHAPTER FIVE

JULIA wiggled her bare toes in front of the lively flames in the wood-burning stove as she sipped the mug of hot coffee that Bernard had just put into her hands before settling himself amongst the squashy cushions beside his son.

'I can do that, Julia!'

'Do what, Philippe?'

She looked across at the other side of the stove and watched as the small boy wiggled his toes much faster than she could. He was curled up in a corner of the old sofa, snuggling up to Bernard, who was looking more relaxed than she'd ever seen him.

She smiled at the pair of them. 'You're much more supple than me, Philippe.'

The young boy giggled. 'That's because I like running about in my bare feet. Maman won't let me go without shoes in Paris but when I come home—I mean to this home, my real home—Papa doesn't mind, do you?'

Bernard put his coffee mug in a safe place on the hearth out of reach of Philippe's arms, which rarely stayed still when he was enjoying himself.

'That just depends on the weather. It wouldn't be a good idea to wade across the farmyard while it's still raining, would it? You saw the state of Julia's jeans and shoes when she came in, didn't you?'

Philippe put his head on one side while he considered his father's words. 'You know, Papa, I think Julia should have taken off her things in the car so she wouldn't have spoiled them.'

'Maybe I didn't want to arrive in the kitchen half-dressed.' She took another sip of her coffee, feeling a nice, warm, thawed-out feeling creeping over her.

'Oh, it wouldn't have mattered, would it, Papa? You see people with no clothes on all the time, don't you?'

Bernard looked across at Julia with a whimsical expression on his handsome face. 'I do indeed, son. But not usually beautiful young ladies like Julia. I have to say, though, that Julia's own trousers are a much better fit. Kind as it was of Marianne to wash them, these baggy jeans tied up with an old belt look most comical on her.'

She gave him a wry smile. 'Oh, very funny! Are you trying to tell me I look frumpish now?'

'Julia, you would look good in an old sack.'

She felt overwhelmed by the admiration that shone from his eyes. She realised he was flirting with her, probably feeling safe because his son was with them.

Philippe was obviously enjoying being part of a grown-up conversation. Suddenly, he jumped up.

'Shall I get a sack, Papa? I know where Gaston keeps a whole pile of them in the barn. We could cut some holes for her arms and then Julia could put it over her head. Then we could all play at dressing-up, couldn't we? Would you like that, Julia?'

She pretended to be considering the offer,

keeping half an eye on Bernard, who looked as if he was going to say something outrageous. Keeping a serious expression on her face, she said, 'I think you might get a bit wet, Philippe, if you go out to the barn.'

'Oh, yes, the rain!' Philippe stared across at the kitchen window where the drops of rain seemed even bigger as they lashed at the panes of glass. 'When will the rain stop, Papa?'

Bernard shrugged. 'Soon, I hope. We'll have to play a game that doesn't involve going outside until the weather improves. Would you like to find one of your board games that the three of us could play together?'

He looked up at Marianne, who'd just returned from organising the washing in the utility room alongside the kitchen and was waiting to say something to him.

'Bernard, I heard you talking about the weather. I was about to suggest we have an early lunch because the weather report says things are likely to improve…'

Julia gathered that the weather report on television had predicted there would be dry weather and sunshine in the afternoon. Marianne had a chicken casserole in the oven, which she could serve up in a few minutes.

'Excellent! Let's have an early lunch.' Bernard stood up and moved across to Julia. 'Be careful you don't trip up in those baggy pants.'

He held out his hand, which she took, not because it was required to steady herself but simply for the feel of those firm, enticingly capable fingers in an off-duty situation. Marianne said she'd laid the table in the dining room. Bernard, still holding her hand, led her down a stone-flagged corridor to the front of the house, which had a good view of the garden.

Philippe skipped along beside her, chattering all the time. She was glad none of the young boy's conversation required an answer because she had suddenly become overwhelmed by the warm feeling of the intimacy that was developing between the three of them. She felt she was enveloped in a family situation that seemed perfectly natural.

'I want to sit next to Julia, Papa!'

'That's strange, so do I.'

'She can sit between us, can't she?'

Bernard led her to the table where a beautifully laundered white cloth had been placed. The silver cutlery shone in the light from the chandelier hanging over the centre of the large round table.

'It's not often we need to have the light on during the day,' Bernard said, glancing out at the darkened garden with low black clouds overhead.

He held out a chair for her. Philippe sat down quickly beside her. Bernard smiled. 'It's a good thing we have a round table. My grandparents bought this table for my parents when they were first married.'

Marianne bustled in and placed the chicken casserole in front of Bernard.

'Enjoy your lunch!'

'Thank you!'

Bernard began serving out portions of the delicious casserole. Throughout the meal the warm rapport between the three of them continued.

The conversation flowed, the food was exceptionally good and only Philippe noticed, as he put down his dessert spoon, preparing to leave the table, that the rain had stopped.

'Papa, the weather report was correct. Here's the sun!'

He waved his arms excitedly at the sun, which was now shining through the windows as they left their places in the dining room.

Julia was feeling replete, having enjoyed a good helping of the chicken casserole and farm-grown vegetables followed by a home-made apple pie. Philippe had enjoyed joining in the conversation and she found she loved the sound of his young voice making interesting comments, asking questions, always giving a positive aspect to what they were discussing.

He seemed older than six but that was possibly because he'd had to get used to different situations during his short life. She hoped Bernard would elaborate at some point about why his marriage had been as disastrous as he'd implied. It couldn't have been his fault. He couldn't have brought about a divorce…not with his generous personality and wonderful parenting skills. His wife must have been in the wrong.

She remembered how, glancing up at Bernard as she'd finished her apple pie, she'd seen him looking at her with an enigmatic expression. Had he any idea how overwhelmed she was by the warmth of the situation they'd created that day, just the three of them? It was the first time she'd felt she belonged somewhere since she'd left her own family home.

Bernard suggested a grand tour of the farm, if he could enlist the help of his son as a fellow guide perhaps? After all, he knew the interesting places as well as his father now that it had become second home to him.

Philippe readily agreed to help his father show Julia around. They started with the barns. The smell of the hay in one barn took her right back to her own childhood.

'My brothers and I had some friends who lived on a farm. We used to spend lots of time there in the school holidays and the barns were wonderful places to play hide and seek in.'

Philippe said children in France also played that game but he hadn't got any friends to play it with when he was here and there weren't any barns in Paris.

Oh, dear! Julia wished she hadn't started talking about her childhood. Obviously, neither Bernard nor his son had experienced the enjoyable if sometimes chaotic family situations she'd had. Once more she thought how sad for Bernard that his marriage had been a disaster. He was a brilliant father.

They walked up the hill to see the sheep grazing on the hillside and talked to Gaston, Marianne's husband, who was mending a wall. The affable, middle-aged man was happy to show them his wall-making techniques and smiled encouragingly at Philippe, who was a willing pupil.

'We'll have you up here, helping me out, when you're a bit bigger,' he told Philippe. 'Would you like that?'

'I'd like to stay here all the time. It's much better here than in Paris.'

As they were going back down the hill, Philippe skipping happily ahead of them, Bernard spoke quietly to Julia.

'You've no idea how relieved I was when Philippe just said he'd love to live here.'

'I'm sure he would. It's a wonderful place for a child.' She hesitated. 'You aren't thinking of…?'

'I'll tell you later.'

Philippe was running back up the hill. 'Papa, Julia, look, there's a rabbit by the side of that wall. Can you see it? Oh, look, there's another one.'

She couldn't help thinking that she didn't want this day to end. How wonderful it would be to spend more time with Bernard and his son. She tried not to think too far ahead. This was a one-off day. A day to cherish and not to look into the future.

Bernard handed her a glass of Kir as they sat together in the conservatory, which was bathed in the evening sunlight. Philippe had gone to bed without protest, being completely exhausted by the activities of the day. But not too exhausted to listen to the bedtime story he'd requested from Julia.

She took a sip of her Kir before placing the glass on the small table beside her wicker chair. 'You know, Bernard, little Philippe fell asleep when I was only two minutes into the story. Doesn't say much for my reading, does it?'

'Oh, I don't know. He was almost asleep when I lifted him out of the bath. I gathered you'd be downstairs in the land of the grown-ups within half an hour. What took you so long?'

She raised an eyebrow. 'Need you ask? Marianne intercepted me to check I had everything I need in the guest room. You are all being so kind. I hadn't intended to stay but you both convinced me I had to.

'Then there was your son beseeching me to have breakfast with him and you telling me that you didn't want to drive back to the hospital and… I could have got a taxi, you know.'

'I know,' he said languidly. 'But I wanted you to stay and I got the casting vote.'

He moved his chair closer to hers. 'I wanted to have time to talk to you in an off-duty situation. I don't want to think about the hospital tonight. And…well, I just wanted to be with you. I like being with you.'

He leaned across and cupped her chin with his hands. Slowly, he lowered his head and kissed her on the lips, a long, lingering, deliciously wicked kiss.

As he drew back she reflected that she would have preferred the kiss to have lasted much longer, but that would do for now. It had whetted her appetite for more, more of…well, more of everything where that had come from. But she conceded it really was not part of the plan for a new start in life. Except men like Bernard wouldn't wait for ever while she achieved all her ambitions and then told him he was definitely the man for her.

'What are you thinking?' he breathed.

She looked up into his expressive hazel eyes.

For a brief moment she longed to tell him. To ask him if he could possibly understand her yearning to start a relationship with him whilst having to cope with her sensible reluctance to change her ambitious plans. She couldn't have it both ways...or could she?

She hesitated before moving on from her impossibly romantic thoughts. 'I was thinking how peaceful it is out here. This afternoon you said you were glad Philippe loves this place. Are you planning he should spend more time here?'

He leaned back in his chair. 'The fact is, the situation has been rather thrust upon me. Gabrielle is going to marry Frederic, a rich, retired businessman much older than she is. He's got grown-up children and finds Philippe too much trouble when he's around their Paris house. Gabrielle has asked me to have Philippe to stay with me permanently.'

'But that would be good for you, wouldn't it?'

He gave a big, contemplative sigh. 'It is my dearest wish to have my son living with me. There are a few problems to be sorted before we can go ahead. Gabrielle, of course, is anxious to be able to get on with her wedding plans without having to think about what to do with Philippe.'

'But surely, as his mother… I mean I don't understand. Bernard, you've hinted that your marriage was a disaster but you haven't told me why. Is your ex-wife to blame for…?'

'I should never have married Gabrielle. She was totally wrong for me right from the start and for that I blame myself.'

He splashed some more iced water in his pastis and raised it to his lips, the ice clinking as he took a much-needed drink. If he was going to be seeing more of Julia in an off-duty situation then he owed it to her to fill her in on his background. She was watching him now with a wary expression on her face, as well she might if she suspected half of what he was going to tell her.

He trusted her implicitly. He didn't know why because he hadn't known her for very long. But it was long enough to know she was his kind of woman. Whereas Gabrielle certainly was not and never had been.

He leaned back against the cushions and stared up at the ceiling where a fan was whirling round above his chair, bringing welcome cool air to the warm evening.

'My only excuse for even talking to Gabrielle was that I was young and inexperienced. I met Gabrielle Sabatier in Montmartre. I'd gone with a crowd of fellow doctors to celebrate the fact that we'd all qualified in our final exams. Gabrielle was working as a waitress in the restaurant where we were having supper. She told me later that evening...' he paused as a sudden vivid recollection of that seedy flat in a narrow street forced itself upon him '...that she needed a wage to pay her rent while she was searching for employment as an actress, having just finished drama school.'

He got up and walked over to the window, looking out across the lovely garden so lovingly cared for by Marianne and Gaston, and beyond the garden wall the hills bathed in evening sunlight. He'd always loved beautiful things in his life. How could he have fallen victim to the tawdry life that Gabrielle had introduced him to?

Julia moved swiftly across the room and stood in front of Bernard, looking up at him, her eyes full of emotion as she recognised he was undergoing some sort of crisis.

'Bernard, you don't need to tell me about your past life if it distresses you. Come and sit down again.'

'If only…' He enfolded her in his arms, bending his head so that their cheeks were together.

She could feel the dampness of his cheek as he struggled to contain his emotions. She remained silent for a few seconds, feeling his heart beating against hers, experiencing a longing she'd never known before.

And then he kissed her with an urgency that thrilled her through her whole being. This was the man for her, with all his past problems, with all his future ahead of him to sort out which way he would turn. She longed to be a part of his life.

Gently he released her from his arms and stood

looking down at her, the evening sunlight bathing the two of them as if blessing their emotional embrace.

'Julia, I want to tell you everything about my liaison with Gabrielle. Things I've never discussed with anyone before. I feel…I feel you will understand why I have such a lot of emotional baggage to contend with.'

He took hold of her hand and together they walked back to their seats. He settled her and moved his chair even closer. She took a sip from her glass and he reached for the bottle of crème de cassis to top her glass up.

'You see, I'd never met anyone like Gabrielle in my life. I thought I'd fallen in love with her even while she was serving on at the crowded table in Montmartre. My friends were joking, saying she fancied me. Well, I was overwhelmed by this vivacious, sexy creature, as were all my friends.'

Julia couldn't help jealous vibes disturbing her. Oh, dear, she was becoming more involved than she'd ever meant to be. Maybe she should insist he keep it all to himself? His past was something she didn't want to think about.

'Gabrielle asked me to wait until she'd finished work and go back to her flat with her.' He paused and drew in his breath. 'I knew what would happen. I wanted it to happen. Yes, we became lovers that night and I was too enamoured to see what she was planning.'

'Which was?' As if she couldn't guess!

'She thought I was a good catch. A young doctor with a safe, well-paid career ahead of him. A meal ticket for life! Sorry, I don't want to sound bitter but...anyway, weeks later when she told me she was pregnant, like the idiot I was, I agreed to marry her.'

Julia felt a pang of sympathy for the young, inexperienced Bernard. She leaned across and squeezed his hand. 'It often happens to young men, even experienced men.'

He flashed her an endearing smile of gratitude. 'I hope Philippe has more sense when he starts growing up. Anyway, it transpired she'd been brought up in relative luxury in the sixteenth arrondissement of Paris, in between the Bois de Boulogne and the river Seine—in a very pricy house. Her father had been a successful businessman until he overextended himself, went bankrupt and took an overdose, after ensuring that his widow would keep the house, albeit living a frugal lifestyle with Gabrielle, her only child.'

'Did you ever think that Gabrielle had been traumatised by the death of her father?'

'Oh, I'm sure she was. Her response to the tragedy had been to turn herself into an even harder, more ruthless character. But I didn't know that when I agreed to marry her.'

He splashed more water into his glass as he tried to remember exactly how it had been. Julia was right in saying that Gabrielle must have been traumatised by the suicide of her father.

'Believe me, I've made so many allowances for her behaviour…but each time she disappointed me with her responses. Anyway, a few weeks after we were married Gabrielle told me she'd miscarried. I insisted on taking her into hospital where tests proved that she'd never been pregnant in the first place. She knew I'd seen through her plan. We became like strangers when we were together. She began to show her true colours, nagging me to rent a house in the prestigious area where she'd grown up and her mother still lived. I told her I couldn't afford it. I was at the very beginning of my medical career, working all hours I could, and I couldn't take on any more expense. I was exhausted most of the time.'

There was a sound of someone coming down the corridor. Bernard sat up his chair as Marianne appeared in the doorway.

'I'm going to prepare supper for Gaston now, Bernard. You're absolutely sure you don't want me to cook supper for you?'

Bernard smiled. 'We're not hungry yet, Marianne. I'm going to make an omelette and salad later on.'

'Well, if you're sure.' Marianne turned to Julia. 'I've put your jeans in the guest room. I do hope you have everything you need in there.'

'Thank you so much, Marianne, for everything.'

'You are most welcome. See you tomorrow.'

As the footsteps receded down the corridor Julia asked Bernard where Marianne lived.

'She and Gaston live in the old surgery at the end of the house. After my father died we had it converted for them so they could be on site while I finished my schooling and moved to Paris to train as a doctor.'

They were both silent as Julia digested this information, thinking to herself that Bernard hadn't had an easy life. Perhaps that was one reason why he'd fallen in love so easily and so quickly with someone who'd appeared on the surface to be the girl of his dreams.

'So what happened after Gabrielle knew you'd seen through her machinations?'

'Oh, she started to make my life hell. There was I, trying to establish myself as a reliable junior doctor at the hospital and she just never stopped nagging while I was with her. I tell you, I was tempted to walk away from this disastrous marriage but I decided the honourable thing to do was to stick it out. In our family background marriage was a lifelong contract, not to be broken.'

'Didn't she work?'

'She got a small part in a TV soap and told me she'd got a long contract. But actually it was only for three months, to be reviewed. On the strength of that I gave in to her demands that I rent the house she wanted. We moved into the house. Two weeks later Gabrielle admitted her contract had been terminated. I phoned her director to enquire what had happened. He said she was temperamental and unreliable. Hah! What a wise man. If only I'd had the sense to see through her earlier.

'Anyway, I continued to work long hours and began to climb the career ladder. I was earning more and just able to scrape the rent together. Then one day when I returned home there was a note saying she'd left me.'

'How did you feel about that?'

He looked across and smiled. 'If I'm honest,

I felt relieved. It was as if a burden had lifted from my shoulders. I assumed she'd met somebody…and I was right. But two months later she returned. She'd had an affair with a married man who'd promised to leave his wife but he'd gone back to her. She begged me to forgive her. I was too busy with my all-absorbing work at the hospital to contemplate divorce.' His voice dipped as he resumed a tone of resignation. 'I took her back.'

'Was she grateful?'

'She seemed to have changed. She even turned on the charm. I should have realised she was up to something. She began begging me to make love to her. I insisted she stay on the Pill. A baby at this stage of our fragile relationship would have been unthinkable.' He breathed out. 'And guess what?'

'She stopped taking the Pill and became pregnant?'

He gave her a wry grin of resignation. 'Why weren't you there to say that when I took her back! I saw right through her but it was too late.

It was the last straw. Even though I'd always longed for a family, I knew I couldn't afford the added expense unless I earned more. I told her I was going to apply for a prestigious surgical appointment in St Martin sur Mer. If I was successful we would move there.'

'How did she feel about that?'

'She said she wouldn't leave Paris. I told her that if I was successful in getting this appointment I would support her and the baby, whether she came or not. When I told her I'd been successful she flounced out and went to live with her mother but not until after she'd demanded a large monthly sum to be paid into her bank account. The one good thing that came out of her move back to her mother was that there was a steadying influence in her life. Veronique Sabatier is a saint! How on earth she came to give birth to a daughter like Gabrielle I cannot imagine.'

'So Philippe has had a good grandmother to care for him?'

'Absolutely! What a relief. As soon as he was

born I loved him with the all-consuming love that only a parent knows. And now...'

He spread his hands wide. 'I'm going to be able to have him with me always—well, until he's a grown man and leaves the family nest.'

She saw the loving expression in his eyes as he drew her to her feet, holding her close to him. 'Thank you for listening to me. I've never told anyone the full story of my disastrous marriage.'

And then he kissed her, this time more slowly, taking time to savour the joy of being with her. Neither of them was thinking beyond the next moment. The present was all that mattered.

He released her from his embrace, looking down at her with an expression of love on his face.

'Let's go and have supper together,' he said, his voice husky as he struggled to come to terms with the fact that all he wanted to do was lift her into his arms and carry her upstairs.

He put his arm around her as they walked towards the kitchen. She revelled in the connection that existed between them, wondering at how much their relationship had developed during the day. How much more could it develop before she found herself hopelessly in love and unable to sort out her conflicting emotions?

CHAPTER SIX

JULIA lay back against the goosedown pillows. She'd been able to tell it was goosedown as soon as she'd laid her head on the softness that had moulded itself around her head. Mmm. Everything about this room was luxurious, well appointed, but probably rarely used—she hoped! The idea of Bernard having a guest room like this made her think that he wanted to impress the girls he showed in here.

But then did he leave them here all by themselves to admire the room? Almost as soon as he'd shown her the superb bathroom, fluffy towels and expensive soap he had left!

But not before that goodnight kiss. Her legs began to feel weak again, even though she was now lying down. She'd been hanging on to her excited emotions, trying hard not to show her real feelings because she knew she simply couldn't have controlled her desire to make love with him.

When he'd taken her in his arms once more, just outside the door to her bedroom, she'd gathered her thoughts together in something of a panic. She'd wanted him physically, desperately, but her rational self had told her not to go there, not to upset the relative calm of their relationship, which worked with the current situation of professor and student. She'd made mistakes before when she'd allowed herself to give in to her passionate nature.

Yes, he'd kissed her gently at first and her wickedly fluid body had reacted with instinctive longing. Oh, yes, she wanted this man… oh, so desperately. But almost as soon as he'd started to kiss her with real urgency he'd pulled away and whispered, 'Goodnight, Julia,' in that deep, sexy voice. And before she'd known what had happened he had been striding away from her to his own room.

* * *

Shortly afterwards, in his room not too far away, Bernard, lying back against the pillows, was wondering why he hadn't stayed to make love with Julia, cursing himself for doing what he'd considered to be the right thing. He remembered how she'd felt in his arms. She'd given every indication that she'd wanted him to make love to her. He hadn't misread the signals. Would it really have complicated their relationship too much at this stage if he'd given in to his true feelings?

He rolled onto his side, waiting for the waves of desire to calm down. The cold shower he'd just taken hadn't helped as much as he'd hoped. He'd only known Julia a few weeks but he knew that he was falling in love. Being in love with a student—any student—wasn't an easy situation to be in.

Yes, they were both adults, so there was nothing untoward about the situation. Nothing that the hospital board of governors could possibly frown upon so long as they were discreet. It was more the problem of handling the emotion for the next few months before Julia finished the course and took the final exams.

For the final month he would find it easier. With the exams over he could relax. He would already have assessed her performance as a student during the course. A panel of external examiners would mark the exam papers and listen to her answers to their questions in the viva voce exam.

Thinking rationally, as he hoped he was doing now, helped to sort out his confusing thoughts. He realised she was the most talented student he'd ever had to deal with. He mustn't do anything to put her off track because she was obviously very ambitious and had a lot to live up to, coming from a prestigious family background like hers.

There was also the problem of her having been hurt by that dreadful ex-husband who seemed to have been hell bent on destroying her confidence. Since she'd arrived here, he'd been trying to build up her confidence again so she could realise her full potential.

Yes, he'd seen her blossoming into an excellent surgeon, relaxing with her fellow students and having an easygoing friendship with him. She already seemed to be more in control of her own life. He'd admired her when she'd first arrived but this increasingly self-confident woman was becoming more and more irresistible to him.

He turned on the bedside light again, knowing that it would be impossible to sleep, with Julia only a short distance away. The moon was shining through the open window onto his huge bed where he should have brought Julia if he'd given in to his true feelings. He gave an audible sigh as he wondered if she was lying awake staring at this same moon and if so, what was she thinking?

He'd been flirting with her all day so why did he have to rationalise himself out of going ahead with his natural instincts? He didn't even know how she would have felt if he'd suggested she sleep with him. As he'd held her in his arms on the pretence that he had simply been saying goodnight she'd been so wonderfully pliant. He'd felt every curve in that vibrant body reacting to his caresses. But he'd forced himself to leave her.

With the occasional dalliance making his off-duty time more interesting for a while he wouldn't usually have thought twice about making it obvious he wanted to sleep with her. If the woman was willing, they would go ahead. But it didn't mean anything. It was an experience that they both enjoyed as mature adults free of any committed relationship. He'd always checked that they weren't involved with a partner.

But Julia was special, the most wonderful woman he'd ever met. The only woman in his life who made him feel that he had to sacrifice his own feelings so that he wouldn't spoil her future potential. She was like a precious flower that he had to nurture.

The sun was shining in through the gaps in the chiffon drapes at her window. Julia stirred and cautiously opened her eyes, unsure of her surroundings. She'd lain awake half the night but the sleep that she'd just been enjoying had been very deep and she was reluctant to return to reality. Somewhere in a nearby room she could hear a child's voice singing.

So, she hadn't dreamed she was in Bernard's farmhouse. She hadn't imagined that wonderful day they'd spent together.

She sat up quickly as she heard gentle tapping on her door.

'Julia, can I come in?'

'Of course, Philippe!'

She pulled the robe from the bedside chair to cover her shoulders. Even as she did so she remembered how impressed she'd been when Bernard had produced the cream silk, extremely feminine robe last night. But then the inevitable moment of jealousy as to who'd worn it before her had threatened to invade her happy mood.

Philippe stood beside her bed, smiling. 'Marianne has sent me to tell you that breakfast is ready.'

The young boy described the delicious breakfast that Marianne had prepared and Julia listened, smiling at him. She raised her head as she became aware that Bernard was now standing in the doorway. He was wearing a dark blue towelling robe that covered most of him except for his athletic, muscular calves and bare feet. His dark, sleep-tousled hair was still damp from his shower and he was looking wonderfully handsome with the sunlight on his lightly tanned face.

'No need to hurry, Julia. I've brought you some coffee. Marianne is still making preparations downstairs so take your time.' Bernard placed a small tray with a cafetière and a delicate porcelain cup and saucer on her bedside table. 'Philippe insisted it was time to wake you.'

'Julia was awake when I knocked on the door, weren't you?'

'I was indeed, Philippe.'

Her eyes met Bernard's over the top of the small head and she felt her heart turn over. The warmth and love she'd felt yesterday had returned as she became wrapped up once again in this idyllic family situation.

Bernard retreated again to the doorway and

held out his hand towards his son. 'Philippe, come with me while Julia gets herself ready.'

'Can't I stay and run her bath for her, like I do for you, Papa?'

'I think Julia will be happy to have a few quiet moments to gather her thoughts for the day ahead, so we'll see her when she comes downstairs.'

After they'd gone, she enjoyed a leisurely soak in the bath, balancing the delicate coffee cup in the small tiled alcove of the wall. It made a welcome change from the hurried shower she took most mornings in her tiny en suite.

When she got herself downstairs fully clothed in her workout gear from the previous day, the smell of freshly baked croissants drew her to the kitchen. Bernard was reawakening the dormant flames in the wood-burning stove. He closed the stove door and turned as he heard her coming in.

He put down the poker on the hearth and came across to pull out a chair for her at the table. Philippe ran inside from the kitchen garden and jumped up onto the chair beside her and began to eat enthusiastically. He urged Julia to join him and, smiling, she reached for a still warm croissant.

Julia was halfway through her croissant, spread liberally with the home-made apricot jam, when she saw Bernard answer his mobile.

'Bernard Cappelle.'

She saw him frowning. From the ensuing conversation she gathered it was an urgent call from the hospital.

'Of course. I'll be there as soon as I can.'

He looked across the table at her. 'That was Michel Devine from the emergency department. There's been a road traffic accident on the motorway, involving several vehicles. He's asked permission to call in as many of my students as possible to help with the patients who will be treated at the hospital. Are you willing to…?'

'Of course.' She was already pushing back her chair.

'Michel, I've just spoken to Dr Julia Montgomery and she says she's available.'

* * *

Minutes later they were driving down the hill towards St Martin sur Mer. Bernard had asked Marianne to take charge of Philippe, who would have to stay at the farm for another day. Philippe had been delighted at the prospect of a whole day with Marianne and Gaston on the farm and another night with his father.

Julia could see a couple of ambulances arriving outside the hospital as Bernard carefully negotiated his way through the traffic at the foot of the hill. The porter in charge of the hospital gateway directed several vehicles to the side so that Bernard could come through and park.

Inside, Michel was organising his staff. A triage system was being set up so that patients were assessed as soon as possible after their arrival.

A nurse was handing out white coats to the arriving medical staff. Julia pulled hers on and reported to Michel Devine for instructions. He asked her to check out the patient in the first cubicle.

'The paramedics have put a tourniquet round his bleeding leg to stem the flow but we need to do something more effective now we've got him here,' he told her tersely. 'There's a nurse in there who'll help you while you assess what needs to be done, Dr Montgomery. It's obviously a serious orthopaedic problem, which is in your field of expertise.'

She moved through the curtain to the cubicle and went in to take charge of the situation. The young man's eyes pleaded with her to help him as she took hold of his hand. He was lying on his back, his hands clenched over the bloodstained sheet that covered him.

She spoke to him in French, making her voice as soothing as she could. He was obviously in deep shock. Glancing down at the notes the nurse handed to her, she saw that his name was Pierre. She noted that sedation that had already been given at the scene of the traffic accident.

Gently peeling back the sheet that covered his injured right leg, she could see that this was a very serious problem. The right leg had been badly damaged and would require immediate surgery. She was already making a swift ex-

amination of the damaged tibia and surrounding tissues when she sensed that someone else
had joined her in the cubicle.

Relief shot through her when she heard
Bernard's voice behind her. He moved to her
side and leaned across the patient so he could
form his own opinion.

'I'll make arrangements for immediate surgery,' he told her.

She nodded in agreement. 'Are those Pierre's
X-rays?'

Bernard was already flashing them up on the
wall screen. She swallowed hard as she tried to
make sense of the crushed pieces of bone. From
the knee downwards, the leg seemed to resemble
a jigsaw puzzle. Was it still viable? It was going
to require some expert surgery and after-care if
their patient was to be able to walk on it again.
Maybe amputation followed by the fitting of a
prosthesis might be the only option. A decision
would have to be made during surgery.

She held Pierre's hand as Bernard made a swift
call to the surgical wing.

'*Ma femme*, my wife,' the young man whispered. 'Monique. *Je veux*...' His faint voice trailed away as tears started trickling down his bloodstained face.

Even as Pierre was asking for his wife, the nurse, at the other side of the cubicle, was looking directly at Julia. 'The information is in the notes, Doctor.'

Glancing briefly down at the notes, Julia learned that his wife, who was seven months pregnant, had been unconscious since the accident. She'd been sitting beside Pierre in the passenger seat when the vehicle had crashed through. Their patient had cradled her in his arms until a doctor had arrived and taken her away in the first ambulance. She was already in the obstetric suite, undergoing an emergency Caesarean.

'Julia, I'd like you to assist me. Theatre Sister is making preparations for us.' Bernard went on to instruct the nurse about premedication for the patient. Julia was glad he was cool and calm because she knew that was how she must be—totally professional so that she could do her best for the patient.

Bernard came across to speak to Pierre, explaining the serious condition of his leg. Julia held her breath as the subject of possible amputation was broached. Pierre looked at her and then at Bernard.

'Is that a possibility? Can't you…?' His voice trailed away.

'Pierre, we'll do all we can to save the leg, but if it's too badly damaged it would make more sense to amputate. Prostheses these days are excellent and you would be taught to walk. I hope it won't come to that but the decision can't be made until we find the full extent of your injuries. Do you understand?' he added gently.

Their patient closed his eyes for a moment. Then in a clear voice he declared that he fully understood and would accept their decision, whatever it was.

Carefully, Julia withdrew her hand from the patient's grasp. 'I've got to leave you for a short time, Pierre. You'll soon be going to sleep but

I'll be up there in Theatre with you and I'll see you when you come round from the anaesthetic.'

'*Merci*,' he whispered. 'Thank you, Doctor.'

She swallowed hard to force herself to be totally professional, aware of his sad eyes on her as she followed Bernard out of the cubicle.

There was no time for a break during the day. Julia assisted Bernard with Pierre's long operation and found herself scrubbing up for the next patient almost immediately. They were supported by a good team from the surgical orthopaedic department, each member adding their expertise to the operations that were performed.

In the early evening, when she and Bernard could finally take a break, he drew her to one side for a quiet debriefing. They were still both in theatre greens up in the recovery room, having just despatched their final patient to one of the orthopaedic wards.

As Bernard started to speak she sank down onto a plastic chair at the side of the water cooler and reached out to take a plastic cup.

'Here, let me do that for you.'

'Thank you.' She flashed him a grateful smile as she took the cold water from him.

Their hands touched and she felt a frisson of energy running through her at the contact. She drank deeply and didn't stop until she'd finished all of it.

'That's better! I feel almost human again.'

Bernard smiled. 'Michel just called to say the emergency department has dealt with all the accident patients that were assigned to this hospital. He's very grateful for our help and suggests we go off duty.'

'Well, if you're sure they can cope, I'd love to go off duty.'

'I'm absolutely sure. Besides, you look completely whacked, Julia.'

'Thanks very much! That's just what a girl needs, to be told she looks as exhausted as she feels. Still…' She sat upright, threw the plastic cup into the bin and stood up. 'There's nothing that a shower and a change of clothes can't put right.'

'How about supper? That would be reviving, wouldn't it?'

What exactly was he suggesting? She couldn't do anything to stop the anticipation running through her.

'Well, what do you say, Julia? Why don't you come back to the farm with me? I've got to return there as soon as possible because Philippe will be getting impatient. If you're with me, he'll be over the moon.'

He was waiting for her answer. She was very tempted at the prospect.

'Well?'

'Why not?' She didn't like the sound of her breathless voice, which completely gave away her confused emotions. She'd meant to sound so cool, as if this was just an invitation to a friend's tea party.

'Good! I'll call Marianne and tell her you're coming so she can get your room ready.'

'Oh, there's no need to—'

'Yes, there is! Because if you think I'm driving back to the hospital again, you're mistaken.

And don't start talking about taxis. There aren't any out in the countryside. This isn't London or Paris, you know.'

She laughed and suddenly it was as if the sun had come out from behind the clouds. They'd been in a windowless theatre all day but she could almost breathe the vibrant country air that she would experience when they escaped together.

He put a hand in the small of her back. 'Can you be ready to leave in half an hour?'

'I'll try. I've got to spend a few minutes in Intensive Care with Pierre. I promised I would when he came round from the anaesthetic at the end of his operation.'

'I'll come with you to make sure you don't stay too long. The intensive care staff are experts, you know, and the orthopaedic staff are also checking on our patient.'

'Oh, I know he's in good hands but a promise to a patient is a promise.'

He bent down, cupping her face in his hands and kissing her gently on the cheek. 'You're not becoming emotionally involved with a patient, are you, Doctor?'

She felt a fluttering of desire running through her body. That was only a chaste kiss, for heaven's sake. She moved to one side as the swing door opened and a nurse walked in.

'We can continue this discussion as we go along to see our patient,' Bernard said gravely, leading the way out into the corridor.

Sister in Intensive Care gave them a brief update on Pierre's condition as soon as they arrived. He was on continual intravenous infusions of blood and breathing normally now after the initial difficulties following the general anaesthetic.

'It was a long operation,' Bernard said. 'Has he asked for details?'

'He's still very confused and the morphine keeps him semi-sedated. But he'll be pleased to see you so that you can explain what you actually did.'

Julia picked up the notes. 'Let's go and see him.'

Pierre's eyes were closed and he was lying on

his back. His injured leg was up on pillows, covered by a cradle.

'Pierre,' Julia said gently.

Their patient opened his eyes and a slow smile spread across his face.

'Thank you,' he whispered. 'You did save my leg, didn't you?'

'Yes, we did,' Bernard said.

'And my wife, *ma femme*?'

Sister smiled broadly. 'I was just coming to tell you. I've had a call from Obstetrics. You have a beautiful little daughter, Pierre. She's very tiny because of being premature so she'll need to stay in hospital for a few weeks.'

'*Et ma femme?*'

'Monique is very weak so she'll be staying in hospital for a while until her strength returns.'

'You'll all be in hospital for a while,' Julia said. 'We'll arrange who can visit who as soon as possible.'

Pierre breathed a deep sigh of contentment. 'You've all been so good to us.'

* * *

As they walked back down the corridor and out through the front door, Julia looked up at Bernard. When they'd left Intensive Care he'd waited while Julia popped back to her room to change and pack some nightclothes. She met him at the hospital entrance.

'It's at times like this I remember that I love being a doctor,' she said quietly, lengthening her stride to keep pace with him.

He took hold of her hand as they continued walking towards the car park.

She glanced around to see if anyone was watching.

'Don't worry,' he said, as if reading her mind. 'We're off duty. We can do anything we like.'

'Anything?'

He grinned. 'Why not?'

CHAPTER SEVEN

As BERNARD drove up the narrow, winding road that led to the top of the hill above St Martin sur Mer, Julia could feel herself relaxing already. She leaned back, studying Bernard's firm hands turning the steering-wheel as he negotiated one of the bends. A white sports car was coming towards them, a young couple laughing together as they passed within inches of their car, driving much too fast on that potentially dangerous section of the road.

Bernard eased off the accelerator just in time as he realised the other car was going to encroach on their side of the road. The blaring music from the young couple's car became fainter as it disappeared down the hill.

He breathed a sigh of relief as he continued up to the top of the hill. 'They wouldn't drive with such abandon if they'd seen the damage that sort of driving can do.'

'I was thinking exactly the same. Michel told me the multiple crash we assisted with was caused by a van driver using a mobile phone as he was overtaking a car. He lost control of his van, ploughed through the central barrier and vehicles piled up around him.'

'Including our Pierre and his wife,' Bernard said quietly. 'I'm so relieved it was possible to save them. The result of good teamwork throughout the day—paramedics, nurses, doctors, everybody.'

He took a deep breath as the enormity of the events finally hit him now that he'd left hospital and was able to assess the situation.

His voice wavered with emotion when he spoke again. 'Pierre and Monique had only been married a few months and that precious baby was a much-wanted child.'

Julia swallowed hard. 'All babies are precious.'

Bernard could hear the gentle, emotional tone in her voice as she said this.

'You love babies, don't you?'

'Yes, of course I do.' She hesitated. 'I'd love to have my own baby. But not until the right time,' she added quickly. 'I need to feel I'm in charge of my own life first.'

He eased the car over the brow of the hill. 'Since you arrived I've sensed you're becoming more and more in charge.' He changed gear as the road flattened out. 'But, Julia, you mustn't be too inflexible. Who was it that said life is what happens when you're making other plans?'

Julia thought for a few moments. 'I don't know who said it but it's very true.'

They were sailing down the other side of the hill now, into the green, spring-awakened valley. She could feel the connection between them growing stronger by the minute.

She clenched her hands as the truth of everything that had happened since she'd met Bernard hit her. This was the sort of man she wanted in her life. She drew in her breath. This was the actual man she wanted in her life. But even as the realisation came to her she reminded herself that the timing wasn't right.

She'd planned to make a fresh start. This was why she'd left the old life behind. She shouldn't be thinking of veering off course. She'd done that before and look where that had landed her!

But she needn't change direction if she was careful. There was no harm in enjoying the present without taking too much thought about the future. She needed the fun and enjoyment of being with Bernard. He lifted her spirits. So, all things considered, she could make her present situation work…couldn't she?

As they drove through the farmyard gates, she determined to enjoy the evening whatever happened. She was going to focus on the present and let the future take care of itself for now.

Bernard switched off the engine and reached a hand across to take hold of hers. 'You're very quiet all of a sudden. What are you thinking?'

'I was thinking about how much I'm looking forward to seeing Philippe.'

A little whirlwind dashed out through the kitchen door, tearing towards the car.

Bernard laughed. 'You've got your wish.'

'Papa! Julia! I was waiting for you to arrive. Marianne! They're here.'

Bernard suggested the three of them have an early supper together at the kitchen table. He explained to Marianne that both he and Julia hadn't had time for lunch and also they both wanted to spend as much quality time with Philippe as possible before he went to bed.

The supper was a riotous success with Philippe excited and happy to have the undivided attention of two doting adults.

'Would you like some more pie, Philippe?'

Bernard was already slicing through the pastry to the succulent guinea fowl underneath in anticipation of his son's answer. Marianne's pie was a family favourite.

Philippe grinned and held out his plate. 'Yes, please.'

'You must have had a busy day to give you a

good appetite like this.' Bernard put a generous slice on Philippe's plate.

'It was brilliant!' Philippe recounted the day's happenings, including feeding the hens, collecting the eggs still warm from the nests, helping Gaston mend a wall and milking the cows.

'And you helped me with the pastry,' Marianne said as she came in with a platter of cheeses from the larder and placed it on the sideboard. 'I'll leave this here, Bernard, for when you're ready for your cheese course. I've also left some desserts in the fridge, if you wouldn't mind helping yourselves. I'm going over to see my sister in the village tonight.'

'Of course, I remember now. It's her birthday. You should have reminded me and gone earlier. Thank you for this excellent supper. Go off and have a great evening.'

Julia came down to the kitchen after putting Philippe to bed to find that Bernard had finished clearing up. The dishwasher was whirring away in the background as he came towards her and handed her a glass of wine.

She gave him a wry grin as she took the glass from his hands. 'I try to stick to the rule that I don't drink after supper if tomorrow is a work day.'

'Ah, rules were made to be broken. This is only a *digestif.* Something to round off a delightful dinner.' He raised his glass to his lips. 'Here's to good food, excellent wine and congenial company.'

She took a sip of her wine, feeling suddenly shy now that they were alone.

'How was Philippe when you left him?' he asked.

'Trying hard not to fall asleep before you've been up to see him.'

He put his glass down on the sideboard. 'Don't go away. Take your wine into the conservatory and I'll be back shortly. And, Julia...?'

'Yes?'

'Don't fall asleep. I know you must be tired but...'

She laughed. 'I've no intention of falling asleep.'

As she settled herself on the comfortable, squashy-cushioned sofa she knew she hadn't felt this happy for a long time. Yes, she would go with the flow again tonight. She'd seen enough misery during the day. She was going to seize the moment and not think about tomorrow. If Bernard held her in his arms tonight as he'd done last night, she was going to make sure that this time she gave him the right message. She wasn't going to let him give her a goodnight kiss and leave her languishing in her lonely bed, thinking about what might have been.

'Philippe's asleep,' Bernard whispered as he sat down beside her on the sofa a few minutes later, putting his arm around her and drawing her against him.

She could feel the instantaneous awakening of her whole body. In the short time he'd been away from her she'd been fighting against weariness. But as soon as she felt his arm around her she was totally wide awake. She could feel every fibre of her body quivering with anticipation as he bent his head and kissed her, oh, so gently. She parted her lips to savour the moment. His kiss deepened.

This was the first time he'd kissed her with such glorious abandon. She responded in equal measure. She gave an ecstatic moan as his hands began to caress her breasts. Deep down inside her she felt herself melting, becoming entirely sensual, fluid, unwilling and unable to control the rising desires inside her.

Suddenly he broke off and leaned back against the sofa. His breathing was ragged as he looked questioningly into her eyes.

'Julia, I want to make love to you so much but we need to discuss what this will mean to our relationship. I'd love to settle into a serious long-term relationship with you but I don't think that either of us could make the commitment necessary. You've got your career to think of and eventually you will want a husband and a family of your own. I'm not sure after my last experience that I will ever be able to offer that to you, and I know that would be a great disappointment to you.'

She hesitated. 'Yes, it would. You have your son. I've always wanted children when I've established my career. My first marriage was a disaster but I adored my stepchildren. It was so hard to walk away and never see them again.'

Her eyes misted over. Bernard moved closer again, taking hold of her hand and kissing the palm very gently. 'I want you to have the experience of your own children because you have so much maternal instinct to draw on. Philippe already adores you.'

'I know. Getting close to Philippe worries me in many ways. Not only will I miss him terribly when the course finishes and I have to return to London, I'm also concerned about him getting used to me being with you. After what he's experienced with his own mother, I'd hate to cause him any more upset.'

'We could have a compromise relationship,

don't you think? A short-term affair while you're here in France?'

He put his arms around her, drawing her closer, his eyes probing hers, willing her to agree.

She gave him a gentle smile. 'I think a short no-commitment affair would be fun. We should live one day at a time, enjoy being together and not think too far ahead.'

'Oh, my darling Julia...'

His lips claimed hers and the passion of his embrace deepened.

Briefly, he paused and looked into her eyes, silently questioning if she wanted him as much as he wanted her.

'Yes, oh, yes,' she whispered.

He smiled, the most wickedly sexy smile she'd ever hoped to see on his handsome face as he scooped her up into his arms.

Julia opened her eyes and for a brief moment she felt unsure of her surroundings as she struggled to leave the dream she'd just enjoyed. Moonlight was flooding through the open window and there was a scent of roses, damp with dew. This room looked out over the garden.

And then she remembered. It hadn't been a dream. The lovemaking had all been real. The gentle caresses that had become more and more irresistible to her. Her own hands had explored that wonderful athletic, muscular body, longing for Bernard to take her completely. And then when she'd felt him inside her she'd felt completely at one with this wonderful man who had been taking her towards the ultimate ecstasy. They had climaxed together in a heavenly experience when they'd clung to each other, feeling that they would never be separated.

'Are you awake?'

She heard his deep, sexy voice from the other side of her pillow. They'd slept together, very, very close. His bed was enormous and there was space all around them.

Gently he pulled a crumpled sheet around her. She realised they were both naked. The rose-scented breeze had probably wakened her.

He raised himself up on one elbow, looking

down at her with a heart-melting expression in his eyes that made her feel she was absolutely special to him.

'Your skin feels chilly,' he murmured, his hands roaming over her in the most tantalisingly erotic way.

For a brief moment she thought he might leave her and go across the room to close the window. But, no, he'd had a better idea!

She moaned with desire as he covered her body with his own. This time their lovemaking took her to heights of ecstasy she'd never imagined existed.

As they lay back against the pillows, their arms still around each other, she could feel her body tingling with the excitement of a joyful consummation.

'Are you still cold?' he whispered.

She laughed. 'I think we should both run barefoot on the dewy grass outside to cool off.'

'You look wonderful when you're totally abandoned. You should stay like this all the time, no problems, no rules...'

'No tomorrow,' she whispered, as she realised they were both longing to make love again…

It was the early morning sun shining in through the still open window that woke her up this time. And this time she knew immediately where she was because she was still clasped loosely in his arms. Mmm, what a night! It had definitely not been a dream. In her wildest dreams she could never have imagined all that. Maybe she'd died and gone to heaven.

So, what now?

CHAPTER EIGHT

JULIA switched off her computer. In the past few weeks since that idyllic night she'd spent with Bernard her life had revolved around work. He seemed intent on working through the syllabus in great detail, with her and the rest of the students using practical sessions in Theatre and theoretical tutorials.

Her mobile was ringing.

'Julia, are you free this evening?'

Was she free? If she wasn't she would make sure she cancelled whatever it was that stood between her and an evening with Bernard. She'd seen precious little of him recently in an off-duty situation and was beginning to think he regretted suggesting a short-term affair. Or maybe he just didn't have the time.

'I'll just check.' She paused just long enough

to flick to the right page in her diary. Totally devoid of any social engagement. 'What did you have in mind?'

'I need to talk something over with you. Actually, I feel I owe you an explanation as to why I've been a bit distant recently.'

He paused and cleared his throat.

She waited. Was he going to explain why he'd seemed somewhat distracted whenever they'd been together?

He sounded unusually nervous when he spoke again. 'It was a pity I had that phone call from Gabrielle so early in the morning when you were staying with me. Having to take Philippe back to Paris that day wasn't what I'd planned but my ex-wife can be very difficult if she doesn't get her own way.'

She waited again as he paused, not wanting to interrupt the flow. She remembered she'd crept out of his bed and gone to the guest room early in the morning before anyone else had woken up. So she'd been surprised when Bernard announced at breakfast he had to take his son back to Paris and had cleared his commitments at the hospital for a couple of days. Michel would be in charge of his students—who, of course, included her—and he would give them on-the-spot tuition in the emergency department.

'Frederic, Gabrielle's future husband, wanted to legally clarify the situation on custody of Philippe, to make sure that he wasn't going to be involved in any way and that I was going to take charge of my son. It's been hell sorting everything out for the past few weeks. I don't know who's worse to deal with, Gabrielle or Frederic. They deserve each other! Anyway, are you free to have dinner with me this evening?'

'Yes…I'd love to.'

No point in hiding her feelings. He sounded much more like the man she'd found so intriguingly irresistible when she'd first arrived.

'Are you in your room?'

'Yes, I've been working.'

'I'll reserve a table at the hotel restaurant for eight o'clock. Meet me in Reception about half past seven.'

* * *

He breathed a sigh of relief as he put the phone down. The past few weeks had been difficult for him. Besides coping with Gabrielle and Frederic's demands, going over to Paris every weekend, he'd also been trying to sort out his feelings for Julia. He'd had to make sure he remained dispassionate about her in his professional dealings. The fact that he'd convinced himself he could handle a short-term relationship before they'd made love that night didn't make it any easier. The practicalities of a relationship between professor and student took some careful handling.

Also she'd had a disastrous marriage. He couldn't be flippant about any relationship that grew between them. It had to be what they both wanted. Now there were other practical considerations. With Philippe's imminent arrival it was going to be difficult for them to see each other. Julia had spoken the truth before as well—if she became an item in his life Philippe would come to regard her as a mother figure. He suspected he already did but to what extent he couldn't be sure. So if she walked out of their lives—as well she might now that her confidence had returned and she was very much in demand—his son's heart could be broken as well as his own!

The fact remained that they ultimately wanted different things out of life. She deserved a husband devoted to her and children of her own. Was he the man to take that risk again? He'd vowed to himself while he was going through the hell that Gabrielle had created during Philippe's early childhood that he would never have another child. Even though he adored Philippe he still remembered the problems associated with having a baby. Could any partnership remain a loving relationship while the parents coped with the problems that babies posed, especially career-minded parents battling with everyday work situations?

He sighed as he went into the shower to prepare for this important date. He'd decided he would stay in the medics' quarters tonight and had brought a casual suit to change into.

* * *

He was relieved to see her welcoming smile when he went into Reception. He'd almost forgotten how beautiful she was when she wasn't shrouded in a white coat or a green theatre gown, or else frowning over a problem that needed explaining in a tutorial. She was wearing some kind of silky-looking cream dress and heels. That made a change from the T-shirt, jeans and trainers that seemed to be standard uniform among his students.

He felt a flicker of desire running through him as he noticed how sexy she looked with the dress accentuating her slim figure yet clinging to the curves of her breasts and hips.

He took a deep breath to steady his emotions as she began to move towards him. She seemed to glide in those strappy high-heeled sandals that made her ankles look so slim. The skirt skimmed her knees, hiding those fabulous thighs, which he knew were oh, so tantalising.

'Julia, you look stunning!'

He rested his hand on the back of her slim waist to guide her out through the door, aware that they were being watched by various members of staff. He would reserve his kiss of welcome till later.

He raised his hand. 'I think that should be our taxi.'

Checking with the driver, he helped her inside. They sat slightly apart on the back seat as the taxi drove off towards the seafront.

Julia could feel her excitement mounting. Glancing sideways, she saw her handsome escort was watching her. She smiled at him. He moved closer, took hold of her hand and kissed her briefly on the lips.

Her fingers tingled as his hand closed around hers. Mmm, they were on course again! She didn't know where they'd been but she knew, or rather she hoped she knew, where they were going.

The hotel was one of the older buildings at the far end of St Martin's seafront. She remembered reading about it in a good-food guide. It certainly looked like a very smart sort of place from the outside.

A uniformed man came to open the car door for her as Bernard was paying off the cab. Inside the ambience was relaxed and welcoming. They were shown into the dining room with a small discreet bar near the entrance. Their table by the window was ready. She sat down, her eyes catching a glimpse of the darkening sky over the sea. The sun had already dipped into the sea and the pink and blue twilight seemed so romantic.

She looked across the table at Bernard, her heart brimming with emotion, feeling so close to him again. He was ordering a bottle of champagne.

'What are we celebrating?'

He smiled. 'The end of an era.'

She gave him a questioning look.

'I'll tell you when the champagne arrives… ah, here we are.' He was glancing at the label. 'Fine. Yes, open it, please.'

The popping of the cork, the fizzing in her glass. She was intrigued, impatient for him to enlighten her.

'Here's to the future,' he said enigmatically,

holding his glass towards hers. 'I've finally set-tled everything with Gabrielle and Frederic but it's been difficult dealing with them. They're going to be married next week and Philippe is safely tucked up in bed at the farm. Marianne is over the moon to have him finally living back home where he should be.'

'So, what was the problem?'

'Problems!' he corrected her. 'Where shall I start? Everything had to be legally sanctioned as regards Philippe. Gabrielle wanted him to be privately educated but I insisted I wanted him to have the same upbringing I'd had out here at the village school. I want him to enjoy the coun-tryside. To bring his friends back to the farm whenever he wants to.'

'What did Gabrielle think of that idea?'

'Well, of course, neither she nor Frederic want to be involved in bringing him up themselves but they wanted him to be taken each day to a private school about twenty kilometres from the village where he would mix with "decent children," was how she described it to me. She pointed out that she wanted him to have the best education possible so he would be a success in life.'

Julia watched him take a drink from his glass, noticing the perspiration on his brow and the set of his jaw as he swallowed hard. It hadn't been an easy time for him, she surmised.

He put down his glass. 'I pointed out that Philippe had set his heart on being a surgeon like me and the village school had given me a good education, preparing me for eventual admission to the excellent lycée in Montreuil.'

'Did that satisfy her?'

'Well, Frederic and I had to convince her that the medical profession was well regarded. She pointed out that we'd had money problems when we were first married. I explained that the early days of a profession are always difficult financially but unless Philippe becomes hampered by a difficult marital relationship—as I was—he would be a success.'

'I bet you enjoyed saying that to her!'

'I certainly did. It also shut her up. She didn't

want me to start making revelations to Frederic of how she'd made my life hell when we were first married. Oh, the poor man doesn't know what he's in for. I actually feel sorry for him. Still, it's not my problem any more!'

He smiled across the table at her. 'Anyway, let's order. What are you going to have, Julia?'

She picked up the menu that the waiter had left with her. She chose moules marinières as a starter, followed by a locally caught fish, with added prawns.

'This is pure nostalgia for me, Bernard. As a child I loved the fish dishes I ate when we were here on holiday—unlike my brothers, who always asked for steak frites.'

'Ah, yes, there used to be a small wooden café on the edge of the beach that served the most delicious steak and chips.'

'That's the one!'

They relaxed into their memories of St Martin sur Mer, which they both agreed had been an idyllic place for children.

'It still is,' Bernard said. 'And the surrounding countryside is the healthiest environment to bring up a child. You've no idea what a relief it is for me to know that Philippe will breathe in clean air every day when he goes to school instead of fumes from traffic.'

'You're very lucky.'

'I am now,' he said, his voice husky.

He reached across the table and squeezed her hand. She felt desire rising up inside her. Did he mean what she hoped he meant?

Their meal was beautifully served. They took their time, caught up once more in their conversation, which flowed so easily.

Bernard told the waiter they would take coffee on the terrace. He took her hand as they went out of the dining room and relaxed in the cushioned wicker chairs by a small table overlooking the sea.

He was intensely aware that this was the first time they'd been alone since they'd made love on that idyllic night they'd spent together. It had been almost too perfect for him. She could be the woman of his dreams, but there were so many reasons why he had to be careful with her.

He took a sip of his coffee. 'You know, you've changed a great deal since you first arrived, Julia.'

'Have I?'

'You've become much more confident and your confidence seems to grow day by day.'

'I'm certainly enjoying the course...in an exhausting kind of way. So much work to get through and then the exams looming at the end of it all.'

'I don't think you need to worry. Hard work plus natural talent for your chosen profession will bring success.' He paused, trying to make his question sound as innocent as possible. 'What have you planned to do after the exams?'

The question, out of the blue, threw her completely. 'Well, I'd planned to go back to London. Don arranged for me to have a six-month sabbatical from the orthopaedic department. I enjoy my work there and it's a good springboard from which to climb higher up the ladder, either in my own hospital or wherever a promotion should arise. I've always been ambitious but…'

He waited, watching her struggle to find the right words. He sensed what she would say even before she spoke again.

'I can't help my longing to have a child, well, a whole family really. And fitting that in with the demanding career I've also set my heart on is confusing. I'm really beginning to appreciate my parents' dilemma. I wonder if I'll have time to fit in everything I want to do with my life.'

He watched her trying to deal with the conflicting thoughts running through her mind. Since telling Julia he wasn't sure about being able to marry again and have more children, he'd had time to think. Marriage and parenting with Julia would be a totally different experience from what he'd had with Gabrielle. If they split the responsibilities fifty-fifty, they could both continue their careers.

But such a situation would require total commitment to each other as well as the child. Marriage really was the only way. But if he told her he'd changed his mind about children and asked her to marry him, would she agree simply to have him father a child? He had to be sure she loved him first and foremost before he thought so far ahead.

That was why he'd needed some space from her after falling so hopelessly in love during that night they'd spent together at the farm. The struggles he'd endured with his ex-wife and her new partner had given him time to think about his relationship with Julia.

She was watching his serious expression. 'You're very quiet. Is something troubling you?'

'No, definitely not. Except…' He took a deep breath, almost frightened to say what was on his mind. His feelings were intense and raw, he could even feel them manifesting themselves in every part of his vibrantly awakening body. Would she feel the same way?

'Will you excuse me for a moment?'

He was already walking back into the dining room. She sat very still. Through the open door she could see him talking to the head waiter and decided he was paying the bill.

Darkness had fallen. She looked out across the bright lights beside the seafront. There were palm trees planted at the edge of the beach, which looked wonderful in summer but took a beating sometimes during the winter.

She was so captivated by the view that she didn't notice him come back to the terrace. He took her hands and drew her to her feet. He was grinning in a boyish, mischievous way.

'I've got the option on the bridal suite for tonight. I thought it would be a perfect place to relax at the end of our busy day. You won't have to creep out before dawn so as to avoid being seen in my bed either. A discreet chambermaid will bring breakfast in bed too, if you'd like. What do you say?'

She giggled. 'I'd say you'd gone mad. Why the bridal suite?'

'Because that's the only room vacant tonight.'

'Oh, don't spoil it. I thought you wanted to lavish loads of money on me because I'm worth it.'

If she only knew! He wasn't going to tell her the real truth—that there actually were a couple of much cheaper rooms available.

'So, you're happy to stay here?'

'I'd love to check out the bridal suite. I've never slept in anything like a bridal suite in my life.'

He put his arm around her waist and led her to the door. 'Who said anything about sleeping?'

She really was confused this time when she awoke in the middle of the night. At first she thought she was in Bernard's bed at the farm. His head was certainly on the edge of her pillow. She put out her hand to touch the thick, dark hair. And then she remembered.

The first and last time they'd spent the night together had been fabulous but this time...! Her body was still tingling with the most consummately passionate experience...or was it experiences? They had been in each other's arms from the moment they'd stepped across the threshold of this sumptuously exotic room.

By the time she'd reached the top of the stairs

with his arm around her waist her legs had turned to jelly. Every fibre of her body had been crying out for his lovemaking, his wonderful, creative, heavenly lovemaking.

He opened his eyes and smiled his slow, sexy smile that told her the night was still young. They had hours and hours before daybreak and reality. When they would both try to come back to earth. But for the moment there was no to-morrow…

Julia said that, yes, she would love to have break-fast in their room when he asked her.

He picked up the bedside phone in one hand and reached for her with the other. 'Oh, no, you don't escape this time. Room service, please. We'd like to order two breakfasts please to room… Oh, great, thank you.'

He put down the phone. 'They knew we were in the bridal suite. We didn't make that much noise, did we?'

She laughed. 'I don't remember.'

'Oh, well, in that case, let me remind you…'

'Not now. What about the chambermaid?'

'Oh, never mind the chambermaid.'

'I'm going for a quick shower.'

'Spoilsport,' he said carefully in English.

She waved a towel at him from the door to the bathroom. 'Your English is definitely improving. You must have a good teacher.'

'And your surgical skills aren't too bad either since you found yourself a good teacher.'

'Sorry, what was that?'

'Not important.'

He settled back against the pillows to await her return, feeling blissfully happy with the way things had gone since his sudden daring idea to take a room here. If he could ever be sure that she really and truly loved him for himself and didn't just regard him as a baby maker, he would ask her to marry him. He'd been very careful to ensure she knew he believed in using a condom. An unplanned pregnancy wasn't what either of them needed.

But what about his dread of going through the early days of a new baby? Even the most loving relationship must be affected. His parents had survived and remained in love, but would he and Julia be able to replicate that when they were both ambitious and in difficult and demanding work situations?

For the moment Julia needed to concentrate on her work at the hospital and her exams. But a little light relief in her off-duty time would help to relax her and prevent too much tension, wouldn't it? He smiled to himself as he heard the taps had stopped flowing in the bathroom. She would soon be back in his bed and he would be able to check she wasn't becoming tense again.

There was a knock at the door. He'd have to wait.

Groaning with frustration, he rose to admit the waiter…

CHAPTER NINE

THE summer was moving along too quickly. As she switched off her computer Julia realised that they were more than halfway through the surgical syllabus that Bernard had set for them.

She got up from her chair and walked across her small room, which was now so familiar. It had become home to her and apart from the occasional night up at the farm this was where she'd lived all the time.

And there'd been that completely heavenly night in the bridal suite! She would never forget that. She was beginning to think it might have been a one-off but she hoped not.

She bent to straighten the sheet on her bed, which was exactly as she'd left it that morning before she'd gone down for a practical tutorial in Theatre. As she leaned across the bed to take hold of the sheet she decided to lie down and take a short break before the evening. It had been a long day, a hot day apart from her time in Theatre when Bernard had insisted the air-conditioning be turned up to full.

She stared up at the ceiling. He'd seemed sort of tetchy today. He often seemed a bit irritable when he was teaching and operating at the same time. She could understand it. She could well imagine how she would feel if she had to do the same. Maybe that would happen when she became a more qualified and experienced surgeon.

The life of a surgeon was a demanding one for sure. No wonder Bernard seemed like two people sometimes. There was the man who could relax when they were together. Ah, she loved him so much when they were alone! But she worried about him when he was working. Was that natural when she wasn't sure where this relationship was going? Worrying about her man with a kind of wifely instinct? Also worrying about his child, who was becoming more and more attached to her every time she saw him?

Her mobile was ringing. Maybe it was Bernard, cancelling their date for tomorrow. It had happened when he'd told her there was an emergency he had to deal with.

'Julia, are you free this evening?'

She sat up, alert and excited by this turn of events.

'Yes; just finished writing up this morning's op. Do you think you could explain that new way you demonstrated of closing up the patient? When I was writing it up just now I—'

'Of course I'll explain but not now. I've just finished so I'm driving home in ten minutes. I thought we could all make an early start together on our day off tomorrow. Can you make it?'

'Yes, but I'll need to pack a bag. Where are we going tomorrow?'

'Oh, let's decide this evening. See you in ten, OK?'

She leapt off the bed and started throwing things into her overnight bag. Typical Bernard! He could be so impulsive at times—like booking them into the bridal suite.

She forced her mind not to think about that particular occasion because she wouldn't be ready in ten minutes if she did. She could think about that later when they were alone in his bed.

He smiled and came towards her as she arrived in Reception.

'Well done! I knew you could do it.'

'Why the rush?'

'No reason. Just impatient to leave my daytime self behind and put on my off-duty persona.'

He put a hand on her back as they walked out towards the staff parking area.

'Ah, so you admit you're a different person in hospital from the impulsive man you can be off duty?'

'Absolutely! Guilty as charged. And to think you noticed!'

'Difficult not to.' She got into the passenger seat.

Bernard closed her door and went round to the driver's side. He started the engine and then placed a hand over hers. 'Which of my person-alities do you prefer?'

She smiled up at him, feeling the familiar stir-rings of desire simply by being close to him.

'Definitely the off-duty man. The other one can be a bit of a temperamental tyrant when he's in Theatre.'

He bent his head and kissed her on the lips. Drawing away slightly he murmured, 'Ah, so you noticed? It's only an act I put on to keep the students on their toes.'

'Well, this student was certainly on her toes today.'

'I noticed. That's good!'

He put the car in gear and moved out towards the front gates. 'So the work's going well, is it?'

'Exceptionally well. If you could give me a few minutes' private tuition tonight on that point I mentioned when you phoned?'

'Oh, I can certainly give you my full attention later on when we're alone.' He changed gear as they began a steep ascent.

She felt her body reacting already to the

thought of the night ahead and she sensed he was in a similar mood. His voice had been definitely sexy as he'd said 'when we're alone'. She couldn't wait for the personal tuition.

Sitting around the kitchen table with the excitable Philippe chattering to her, she relaxed completely.

Marianne had bought mussels from the fish merchant who delivered to the village on Fridays and she'd been delighted when Bernard had phoned to say that Julia was coming that evening. The housekeeper placed the steaming, aromatic dish of moules marinières in front of them now.

'Bernard, I think this is one of Julia's favourite dishes, am I right?'

'Marianne, you're amazing!' Julia said. 'You remembered!'

'Well, it's my favourite, also,' Philippe said. 'May I have that big one there, Papa?'

'Of course!'

Bernard beamed round the table, a feeling of

total happiness descending upon him. This was how every working week should end. Sitting at the table with his son and his beautiful, talented…what was Julia to him exactly? Certainly he shouldn't take anything for granted. There was nothing permanent about the situation, even though he wished it could go on for ever.

He glanced across at her and saw she was watching him with those eyes that sometimes looked so questioning, as if she wasn't sure of something, as well she might be. She was the most wonderful woman he'd ever met but he still couldn't allow himself to think of her as being a permanent fixture in his life. He still felt unsure of the future. There were still so many problems to iron out before he could be sure she would always be there.

Bernard put the pencil down on his notepad. 'So, does that answer your question?'

'Yes it does, Professor. That's what I put in my notes but I had to be sure.'

He gave her a sexy grin. 'So may I forget my

academic commitment to a demanding student and relax again, Dr Montgomery?'

She giggled as he put his arms around her and drew her into their first embrace of the evening. They were still downstairs in the conservatory but they were alone at last with the whole of the night ahead of them.

'Marianne has put your things in the guest room,' he said solemnly.

'Do you think she understands the situation?'

'Well, if she does understand what's going on, she's more clued up than I am,' he said enigmatically.

He took a deep breath. 'Of course she assumes we sleep together at the beginning of the night… well, not so much sleep but… Yes, of course she understands the situation. She also understands that you creep along to the guest room in the early hours before Philippe wakes up.' He hesitated. 'You don't have to do that, you know.'

'I just feel that…it's simpler this way. I don't want to confuse him.'

Bernard drew in his breath. He surmised she

didn't want it to be taken for granted that she would always be there. She'd come out to France to make a new start, hadn't she? That had been her initial idea. Now that she'd found her confidence, she may well decide to spread her wings and fly away at the end of the course. She had the whole of her life in front of her. He must never take her for granted.

He drew her closer in his arms. 'Let's go to bed.'

Their lovemaking had been unbelievably tender. Afterwards he held her in his arms so tightly it had almost been as if he was going to keep her there, safe, in the place she loved to be. But there was something different tonight. She sensed a certain melancholy in the moment.

Bernard lay with his arms around her, trying not to dispel the mood. Their consummation had been heavenly as always but almost immediately afterwards reality had forced itself upon him. This relationship was all too good to be true so far. He wanted to make it go on for ever…but only if that was what she wanted. He couldn't burden her with the question of commitment to him when she was coming up to the difficult weeks before the exams and the end of the course.

And he could definitely not bring up the subject of babies. If he told her he was beginning to think he'd love to father a baby with her, how could he be sure it would be him she wanted or a baby? She could be very loving, but so had Gabrielle been when she'd wanted her own way.

But the wounds of his suffering still hadn't healed properly. The thought of spoiling their idyllic relationship by commitment, pregnancy and a small baby to care for, along with dual careers in surgery, was a very daunting one. Julia had come over to France to make a fresh start on her own. Did he have the right to impose a different kind of life on her? He couldn't bear to spoil the brilliant future that lay ahead of someone so talented.

* * *

Julia woke in the early morning and stretched out her hand under the sheet. Bernard wasn't there. Of course he wasn't. She'd made an early departure from his bed last night. He'd seemed tired, less communicative after they'd made love, so she'd decided to come along here to the guest room to get a whole night's sleep before their day out.

He'd kissed her tenderly, lovingly when she'd explained, but he'd seemed somewhat distant, as if he was standing outside their relationship and being totally dispassionate. Maybe she should have asked him if he was worrying about something but she'd sensed he wouldn't have told her. He could be a very private person when he wanted to be. But she loved him, oh, how she loved every facet of his enigmatic character.

She sighed as she switched on the bedside light. Almost seven o'clock. The little whirlwind would come charging in soon.

Bernard had heard Philippe chattering to Julia in the guest room. He'd woken very early today,

which was unusual. Last night had been wonderful, holding her in his arms, making love to
her, knowing they would be together today. He
wasn't going to worry about where their relationship was going. He would simply accept that
they made each other happy and now wasn't the
time to think too far ahead.

'So where are we going today, Papa?'

Philippe stretched his little arm across the
table. Bernard reached forward and wiped away
some of the jam and croissant crumbs that had
collected on the palm of his son's hand with
his napkin. Then he gave the still sticky hand a
squeeze.

'Would you like to go out in the boat?'

'Yes, oh, yes, let's go in the boat, Papa! Out
to the island?'

As Bernard steered his boat across the sea he
could feel the cares of the past week disappearing. He could hear Philippe chattering happily
to Julia, who was pointing out landmarks on the
now distant shore. She too seemed happy to be

out in the boat, reminiscing with his son about her childhood holidays in this area.

'Oh, we didn't have our own boat,' Julia was explaining to Philippe. 'We didn't live over here in France so my father used to hire one sometimes. My brothers always wanted to steer it and I was always the last to have a go…and then only under strict supervision.'

'What's supervision?'

'It's when a grown-up watches you the whole time you're holding onto the wheel and—'

'Papa, will you supervision me while I'm steering the boat? Or Julia could supervision me, couldn't she?'

Bernard turned, one hand still on the wheel. 'Pass me that wooden box. If you stand on that, I'll supervise you while you hold on to the wheel. At least we've got a clear route ahead of us. Nothing for you to bump into at the moment.'

Julia helped Philippe onto the box and stood at the other side of him while Bernard kept a light hand on the wheel.

'No need to turn the wheel, Philippe. We're going straight ahead towards that island.'

'That's our island, isn't it, Papa?'

'Technically, no, but…'

'What's technically?'

'We don't own it but we're allowed to go there.'

'But we've been there lots of times so we can pretend it's ours.'

Bernard stooped and planted a kiss on his son's head. 'We can pretend anything we like today.'

His eyes met Julia's as he raised his head. He could feel a lump rising in his throat as he saw the wistful expression in her eyes. Did she feel the same way as he did about the day ahead? Just the three of them, pretending to be a family?

As they neared the shore, Julia helped Philippe down off the box again so that Bernard had full control of the boat. As they reached the shallows she took over the wheel, as they'd discussed, so that Bernard could jump out and tie up the mooring rope.

'I always wanted to tie up,' she said to Philippe. 'But my brothers got there first. My father would be steering the boat and my mother holding tightly to my hand.'

'It's more fun being a boy, I think.'

'Well, I did used to think my older brothers had a lot of fun. But I always had fun too.' She was holding the young boy's hand as they stepped barefoot into the shallows, holding their sandals so they didn't get wet.

Bernard was holding out his hand to take their sandals as they reached the shore. They walked up the beach to settle themselves under the shade of the trees. Bernard started bringing their things from the boat.

Philippe was already stripped off and running into the sea. He'd insisted on wearing his swimming trunks from the moment he'd got dressed that morning.

'Come on!' he shouted happily.

'Is the sea warm?' Julia asked as she stripped to the bikini she was wearing under her shorts.

'Very hot, hot, hot. Come and try it.'

'OK, I will.'

Bernard took hold of her hand. 'It's going to be a scorcher today.'

She revelled in the touch of his fingers enclosing hers. 'Last time I was here it rained all day and we played under the trees, wearing our mackintoshes.'

He drew her closer, feeling a frisson of desire at the closeness of her bikini-clad figure. 'How old were you?'

'It was years ago! I don't remember. I...' She glanced at the small boy in the sea. 'We'd better go and supervise Philippe.'

Bernard laughed. 'Supervise seems to be the word of the day. I'm glad there's nobody to supervise you and me today. I'm feeling positively reckless.'

She laughed as, still holding her hand tightly, he set off down the beach.

'If only the rest of your students could see you now, Professor!'

'Papa, there are some little fish nibbling at my toes. Look, look, they're everywhere in the water. Julia, come here, can you see them? What are they?'

'Well, my English father used to call them sticklebacks. My French mother simply called them little fish, like you do.' She wiggled her toes. 'They tickle, don't they?'

'Let's swim, Papa. I can swim, Julia. Watch me!'

One each side of him, he proudly swam out towards the deeper water. 'We won't go too far out,' Bernard said to Julia as they swam alongside. 'Philippe loves swimming but he'd go on swimming till he felt tired. He forgets he's got to go back.'

'Yes, but you always put me on your chest, Papa.'

'See what I mean?'

Bernard's arm brushed against hers. The water further out was colder than nearer the shore but even so she felt a warm glow stealing over her. Just being close to him in any situation was one of the joys of their relationship. Again she found herself wondering how long they could be together like this before decisions about the future had to be made. Well, there were no decisions to be made today. Enjoying the moment was her primary concern.

'Time to go back.' Bernard steered the other two around so that they were all swimming back towards the shore.

Bernard had brought everything they needed for a barbecue. He quickly built up the sides with the large stones they'd gathered and got the fire going underneath before placing the metal rack over it.

'I've never tasted such delicious chicken drumsticks,' Julia said, tearing at a piece with her teeth. She looked across at Bernard, who'd just put more chicken on to grill. 'Mmm, you must be a very experienced chef, sir.'

'Papa always cooks lunch when we come here. Why does lunch taste much better out in the open air than inside, Julia?'

She laughed. 'Good question! I've often wondered about it.'

Bernard dropped some more food on Philippe's plate. 'On this particular island it's because we've all been swimming, which is marvellous for inducing an appetite, and the sun is shining through the trees and we're all happy.'

'And we're going to stay here all night in Papa's tent and wake up in the morning to start swimming as soon as the sun comes up.'

'Oh, not this time, Philippe. I didn't bring the tent. Anyway, it wouldn't be big enough for three of us.'

'Yes, it would! Julia and I don't take up very much room, do we? Well, do we really need a tent? It's warm enough to sleep here under the trees.'

Philippe snuggled up to Julia, wiping his sticky hands on a nearby patch of grass. 'You'd like to stay here, wouldn't you, Julia? I bet you stayed here all night when you were here on holiday, didn't you?'

'No, I'm afraid we didn't. Why don't you just close your eyes now, pretend it's night-time and have a short sleep? You look sleepy to me.'

Philippe stared at her. 'How did you know I feel sleepy?'

'Because you got up very early and you've had a busy day that included a long swim. That's always exhausting.'

She was already tucking a dry towel around the small boy and lowering her voice. He snuggled closer into her side. 'You will wake me, won't you, Julia? I don't want to wake up and find it's all dark and I've missed the rest of the day. It's such a nice day. I don't want to miss anything. Don't leave me, Julia…'

His voice drifted away as his breathing steadied and his eyelids drooped.

Watching her, Bernard felt the urge to put his arms round his two favourite people and keep them here with him for ever. He could build a camp here under the trees and blot out the rest of the world and its problems. What a wonderful mother Julia would make when she had children of her own. But she was also born to be a talented surgeon. He forced himself away from the problem. Today they belonged together and the future was the future, something to think about tomorrow.

He sat down on the sandy, grassy slope and reached towards her, careful not to disturb his son sleeping nearby, visible to them through the long grassy fronds. Lowering his head, he kissed her gently on the lips. His kiss deepened. She clung to him, aware of the poignancy of this tender moment. One day in a family situation with Bernard had made her sure of what she wanted in life—career and motherhood, hand in hand. If she could have both options with Bernard that would be perfect. But there were so many obstacles to clear before that could happen. Could she convince Bernard to take a chance on them?

He was pulling her to her feet, leading her to a shadier spot a short way into the trees.

'It's OK, we can see Philippe from here. He's exhausted so he'll sleep until we wake him up.'

She couldn't dispute that even if she'd wanted to, which she didn't! Her passion and desires were rising up inside her as his hands caressed her into a mounting frenzy of uninhibited love-making.

Only as she felt the onset of her climax did she attempt to stifle the moans that were rising in her throat. She mustn't cry out, mustn't wake the sleeping child…

'Julia, it's time to wake up.'

She opened her eyes to see Bernard kneeling beside her. The sun was slanting down in the sky. She glanced across at the still sleeping Philippe.

'How long have we been asleep?'

He gave her a sexy grin. 'Too long. There's a boat coming over. Look. I've started packing up. Would you wake Philippe?'

As she sat at supper much later that night in the kitchen, she knew she would remember this day for the rest of her life. Whatever happened in the future, the days, months and years of uncertainty stretching ahead of them, she would never forget what a blissful day she'd enjoyed before she had to go back to reality and deal with the problems that lay ahead.

CHAPTER TEN

THE end of the course was fast approaching and exams were looming. Concerned as she was about the state of her relationship with Bernard, Julia was just as worried about her performance in these tests. Succeeding at this course had been her reason for coming to France. Bernard had proved a delicious distraction.

As the warm water from the shower cascaded over her body she allowed herself to look back on those halcyon days of high summer when Bernard had taken her out in his boat to 'their' island. Mostly Philippe had been with them, which was always fun. On two occasions he'd been in Paris for the weekend, staying with his grandmother who was always asking for a visit. So they'd gone alone to the island, sleeping overnight in the small cabin on the boat.

She sighed as she patted herself dry with her towel. For the last couple of weeks it had been nose to the grindstone the whole time, revision for the written exams and preparation for practical theatre work. There wasn't much she could do about preparing for the viva voce where a panel of examiners would ask her questions. Either she would satisfy them with her answers or she wouldn't.

She glanced out of the window as she finished dressing. The branches of the tall oak tree at the side of the hospital garden were being buffeted around by a high wind. The leaves had turned an autumnal gold in the past week and some of them had been blown away already. Here in the hospital, where the air-conditioning had been switched to central heating, she would be warm.

After a quick coffee and croissant in the cafeteria, she made her way along the corridor to the orthopaedic ward to see the patient she was to operate on that morning. This was the part she really enjoyed; meeting with the patient, the human aspect of surgery. When he was anaesthetised on the table the situation would change. Especially this morning when there would be an examiner watching her every move.

'Good morning, Vincent. How are you?'

Her patient, a middle-aged man who looked younger than his age and had told her he still wished he could play football, smiled broadly as she arrived at his bedside.

'I'm good, thank you. But I will be happier when the surgery is over.'

She patted his hand in sympathy, secretly thinking exactly the same as he did. How happy she'd be when the operation was over!

'I just called in to check you're OK about everything. We really do appreciate you giving your consent to allow your operation to be assessed by an examiner and performed by someone who is currently qualified to do the surgery but aiming for a higher qualification.'

'Of course it's my pleasure! I'm happy to be of service to the hospital in any way I can. Professor Bernard explained to me about… Ah, but here he is.'

Julia glanced up and saw that Bernard had joined them. 'Hello, Vincent, hello, Julia. Yes, I've explained the exam situation to Vincent.'

Vincent pulled himself up against his pillows. 'Yes, I know I'm in capable hands. Dr Julia will do my knee replacement, with a more senior surgeon by her side, who I hope will be you, Professor.'

Bernard smiled. 'Yes, that's correct. Theoretically I could intervene and take over if I felt it necessary. But in this case I'm sure that won't happen. I've worked with Dr Julia many times and she is exceptionally experienced and talented.'

Vincent gave him a cheeky grin. 'And also very beautiful!'

The two men laughed together boyishly.

'Without doubt,' Bernard said, his eyes meeting with Julia's. 'Beauty isn't a prerequisite for a surgeon but I think it helps the patient to be cared for by someone beautiful on the morning of their operation.'

To her dismay she could feel a blush rising on

her cheeks as her eyes met his. 'I was just about to check that the results of all our pre-op investigations will be made available to the examiner.'

'You're in charge,' Bernard said solemnly. 'I'll leave you to it.'

She was carrying copies of her patient's notes as she left the ward some time later. Everything was in order. The left knee had been prepared for surgery. The paperwork concluded. The results of Pierre's blood tests were to hand. No problems with his haemoglobin or electrolyte balance. He was a man in excellent health apart from the knee injury, which he'd told her had meant he couldn't play football any more, not even for the local team in his village.

As soon as she walked into Theatre a feeling of confidence and capability flooded through her. She was vaguely aware of a stranger at the back of the room who was obviously the examiner. But there was no reason for that to make any difference to her performance. She'd performed a total knee replacement before. No need to worry about the outcome.

The anaesthetist nodded. Everything was OK with the patient's breathing under the anaesthetic.

With a steady, sterile, gloved hand she took the scalpel she'd asked for from Bernard and made the first incision.

'How did it go?'

She looked up at Dominic, her fellow student, who was walking towards her in the corridor as she tried to slip away for a desperately needed coffee at the end of the operation.

She stopped to chat to him. He looked terribly worried and nervous.

'It went well. No need to worry. You'll be fine. I was introduced to the examiner at the end. He was absolutely charming but he gave nothing away.'

'Didn't you ask him how you'd done?'

'Of course I didn't! Bernard's talking to him now. I needed to get away. You're on this afternoon, aren't you?'

'Can't wait!' he said gloomily. 'Can't wait till it's all over.'

'Have you got a nice, co-operative patient?'

He smiled. 'Oh, she's very nice. Couldn't be more helpful. And I know I can do a good job. I'm just on my way to check on her. Thanks for the pep talk, Julia. Just one more question.'

'Yes?'

He hesitated. 'Will you be staying on in France or going back to England once this course is over?'

She drew in her breath. 'I'm still not sure. My consultant in England is waiting for me to let him know. He's still under the impression I'll be rejoining the orthopaedic firm.'

Dominic grinned. 'And your consultant in France is hoping you'll stay here?'

'No comment! Good luck!'

She turned and walked away. She had to make a decision soon about what she should do. But she was still not sure where Bernard stood on their future and she was afraid to ask. She knew she wanted to continue with her career but she also wanted to continue her affair with Bernard. If he would only put into words how he felt about her. Give her hope that their affair could become more permanent…possibly leading to marriage?

She walked on, head down so that she could think without having to break off and talk to someone. Marriage would be a step too far for Bernard. He didn't want children and she did. Could she persuade him to change his mind about that? But then he might think she only wanted him to father a child, wouldn't he?

She banished the thoughts from her head. If only Dominic hadn't opened up all her doubts and fears about where she and Bernard were heading. Perhaps she should phone Don in London and talk it over with him. And if Bernard was still keeping her guessing she'd book a seat on the train and go back to London. Couldn't do any harm. It might even make Bernard tell her how he really felt about her.

Her confidence about her career prospects continued to grow as the exam period continued.

It had been a couple of weeks since she'd operated on Vincent and he'd made excellent post-operative progress. In fact, the orthopaedic consultant in charge of his outpatient care had told her earlier that day that he'd seen him in his clinic, walking extremely well with the aid of a stick in physiotherapy. The consultant had told her he wouldn't need the stick for much longer.

Yes, she was delighted with the news. And also relieved that the other operation she'd performed under examination, which had been the required emergency operation, had also gone very well.

She'd known that she was theoretically on call for the whole of the examination period except when she was actually doing a written exam, doing an exam operation or taking the viva voce. She'd been relieved that when the actual emergency call had come she'd been well rested after a good night's sleep in her room and ready to spring into action.

As soon as the call had come from Michel in *Urgences*, asking her to go immediately to Theatre where an emergency case and an examiner were waiting for her, she'd felt herself to be on top form. A teenage girl had been rescued from a burning car. Unable to move from the damaged passenger seat, she'd been pulled out by her friends through the side window. Her patient's ankle was badly shattered as part of the engine had smashed through the front of the car, crushing her foot.

Quickly assessing that she would have to pin the ankle to realign the shattered bone, she'd simply got on with the job, hardly aware until later that she'd been examined.

After that, the written exams hadn't caused her any problems. Everything in the syllabus had been covered by the questions, which meant there was a variety of choice.

Her phone was ringing. 'How did the viva voce go this morning?'

'Bernard, I thought you would know more than I do!'

'Well, if I did I wouldn't be asking, would I?'

'And if you did you wouldn't be telling either! Oh, the distinguished panel were very civil, very cool, didn't ask me anything I couldn't answer. All in all I actually enjoyed it.'

'Good! You haven't forgotten the party tonight, have you?'

'Of course not.' She sprang off the bed and dashed over to her wardrobe, flinging wide the door. 'I hadn't forgotten but I'm running late. What would you like me to wear?'

'How about that sexy nightdress you brought with you the last time you were here?'

'Oh, you mean that flimsy bit of silk I picked up in the boutique on the seafront? It's still in the bag it came in, as well you know. One day I'll wear it—when I'm allowed to take it out of the packaging!'

'I thought there wasn't much point when I was only going to take it off as soon as you got within reach.'

She heard him chuckling down the line. That was more like the Bernard she knew and loved. The last few weeks had been a tense time for both of them with little time for frivolous exchanges that had nothing to do with exams.

'I'll drive you over to the farm in about half an hour. OK?'

'Fine! How are my fellow students getting out?'

'I've paid for a minibus there and back. I don't want to have to worry about drunk driving amongst my students. I want everybody to enjoy themselves now that the exams are finished.'

Marianne had done them proud! As Julia surveyed the buffet supper the housekeeper had laid on for them she felt she had to quietly congratulate her.

'Oh, I enjoyed it, Julia,' Marianne said as they whispered together in the kitchen. 'And two of my friends from the village came out to help me.'

'They're the ladies who were serving drinks earlier, I presume? Honestly, Marianne, I would have been out to help you today but I didn't finish my last exam until this morning.'

'Julia, I didn't expect you to help when you've

been so busy at the hospital. Bernard told me you were giving all your energy to the exam. That's why we haven't seen you out here for a while. Philippe was so excited when he knew you were coming. And I'm glad you read his bedtime story before he went to sleep. I'd hoped you'd give him some time.'

'I've missed him so much. I just love him to bits. He's…very special.'

Marianne gave her a searching look. 'He feels exactly the same about you, Julia.'

Julia swallowed hard. She knew the implication was that she shouldn't take that love lightly, that she shouldn't break a young boy's heart. Now that she'd finished her exams, all the emotional problems of her relationship with Bernard had begun crowding in on her again.

'Are there any more of those canapés, Marianne?'

It was Bernard, putting an arm round her waist as he rescued her just in time.

'Lots more in the oven ready to come out.' She raised her voice. 'Gaston, get the canapés out, please!'

'What were you two whispering about?' Bernard handed her another glass of wine as he steered her towards the window seat in the sitting room.

Julia smiled. 'I was congratulating Marianne on the marvellous buffet supper.'

'Oh, she loves having a party here. It doesn't happen as often as she would like. Thanks for putting Philippe to bed. He'd been waiting to see you all day, apparently, and I was too tied up with my guests to help you. I popped upstairs to his room just now and he's out for the count. I don't think we'll hear from him, in spite of the noise, until the morning.'

He wondered if she knew how nervous he'd been feeling when he'd said that. He'd decided, really decided, against all the odds that he was going to tell her how he really felt about their relationship tonight. He found himself holding back on the wine. He wanted to remember this night even if…no, he was going to be positive. He had to know the truth, whatever it turned out to be.

'I want to make a toast, everybody!' Dominic was standing in the middle of the room, raising his glass in the air. 'I think I know I speak for all of us on the course when I say that we've had the best professor guiding us every step of the way. I've learned a lot, rediscovered areas of surgical technique I'd forgotten and grappled with the new techniques Bernard has taught us. Whatever my exam results, I'll always be a better surgeon than I would have been and a much better all-round doctor. So, fellow students, please raise your glasses to Bernard, the finest surgical professor we could possibly have wished for!'

Glasses were raised high. The wine flowed. The conversation turned to what everybody was going to do now it was all over. Most of them were going back to the hospitals that were still holding their jobs open for them. The general consensus was that promotions were imminent if their exam results were good. Others were more pragmatic. They would pick up where they'd left off, happy that they'd had the experience to widen their knowledge of surgery.

'How about you, Julia?' Dominic asked. 'Have you made up your mind at last?'

She cleared her throat. She felt nervous with Bernard standing so close to her, listening to every word she was saying. They'd moved to be with the group in the centre of the room but his hand was still lightly on the small of her back.

'I'm keeping my options open for the moment,' she said quietly. 'I'll have to return to London to discuss my future with my tutor, whatever I decide to do.'

'When will you go?' Dominique asked.

She hesitated. They were all looking at her, including Bernard whose expression was totally enigmatic. They hadn't discussed this and she now wished they had. She hadn't had time…or had she simply been avoiding this conversation?

'Well…I've reserved my seat on the Eurostar tomorrow. I'm going to London for a few days to talk things over with Don.'

Bernard swallowed hard, trying not to convey any emotion at the announcement. He should have known this would happen. This now confident young woman who'd come out here for a fresh start and made such an impression on all her colleagues. She was ready now to fly away and get on with her successful life. She was ready to combine career and motherhood whenever the time was right. And even if he'd told her he'd changed his mind about having a commited relationship again, it wouldn't have made any difference.

She didn't need him to be her husband and father her child. She was so charismatic, so utterly desirable, so talented, so sexy she could take her time in choosing the right partner for herself.

As he watched her fellow students crowding round her, wishing her well in the future, he knew that he'd lost her. She was going back to London tomorrow and she hadn't told him. Just for a few days, she'd said. But once she got back there she wouldn't return. Her colleagues over in London would gather around her, just as her French colleagues were doing now, and Don Grainger would persuade her to return and climb the career ladder under his tutelage.

He had to let her go back to London. He mustn't try to dissuade her. It would be selfish of him to try. She was off the course now. Her reason for being here finished. Her exam results would reach her electronically, wherever she happened to be.

CHAPTER ELEVEN

JULIA breathed a sigh of relief as Dominic finally weaved his way across the farmyard to join his colleagues in the waiting minibus. She thought he'd never go so she could be alone with Bernard and explain why she hadn't told him she was leaving for London tomorrow.

She looked around the room but Bernard had disappeared while she'd been listening to Dominic's endless talking. Where was he?

'Ah, there you are, Bernard.'

He was coming through the door. She smiled and moved towards him but stopped in her tracks when she saw he was carrying her overnight bag.

His expression gave nothing away. 'I think it's best for you to go back to the hospital tonight. You've got an early start tomorrow. I've told the driver of the minibus you'll be going back to the hospital and will be with them as quickly as you can.'

'Bernard, I wanted to explain the situation to you tonight. I'm only going to London for a few days.'

'So you said. I'll wait to hear from you. Let me know your plans when you've discussed things with Don.'

He was moving closer, still holding her bag. 'I'll take you to the coach.'

He really meant it! She'd better go gracefully without trying to explain now. Maybe this was his way of ending their short-term relationship. Perhaps he was relieved to have an excuse to end it so easily.

She'd never thought it would end like this. But she'd never been any good at understanding men. She must have got it wrong again!

Her colleagues in the minibus had started to sing now.

Julia winced at the noise disturbing the peace and quiet of the valley but she needn't have worried. Everyone fell silent as she and Bernard reached them. Dominic made a space on the front seat for her and took her bag. For the sake of appearances she smiled at Bernard. He smiled back but it was a wintry smile that was there to pretend that all was well.

The driver was anxious to get going. Everyone started calling their thank-yous and goodbyes.

She doubted very much that Bernard could hear her saying goodbye to him. He gave a wave of his hand and walked back up the farmyard.

She woke in the early morning of a grey dawn. Even the clouds through the window added to her dark feelings. She stretched out her hand towards the other side of the bed. The sheet was cold. She knew he wasn't there. She'd come back to her room at the hospital. Correction! He'd sent her back to her room.

She propped herself up on her pillows and checked the time. She'd set her alarm when she'd got back last night. It would soon be time to get up and make final preparations for the journey.

She remembered the awful journey in the minibus last night. Her friends had become mercifully quiet after she'd joined them. They'd had the decency not to ask questions and they hadn't sung any more. But she'd been very relieved to get to her room and close the door on her own little sanctuary.

Her alarm was sounding. Time to get up. She threw back the duvet. She'd asked the hospital domestic staff to keep her room for a further week until she got back from London. But now she was unsure whether she would return. Her emotions were in turmoil and now wasn't the time to try and sort them out. She determined to go back to London to make her decision.

CHAPTER TWELVE

SHE stepped down from the Eurostar at St Pancras, marvelling at the speed with which she'd been transported from Calais–Frethun. Only an hour ago she was stepping on the Eurostar in France and now here she was making her way through the crowds, hearing English voices. She got a taxi after only a short wait and gave him the name of her hospital.

'Are you visiting a patient?' he asked her conversationally.

'No.' She climbed into the back seat.

Usually she enjoyed chatting with cab drivers as they struggled through the London traffic jams but today was different. She felt different, spaced out, unreal. Maybe when she was back amongst her colleagues in the orthopaedic department she would be able to make sense of her future. She'd gone away with such high, ambitious hopes. She hadn't been looking for an all-consuming relationship that had turned her world upside down and forced her to examine her dreams.

She wished she'd been able to say goodbye to Philippe. She forced herself to ignore her feelings of guilt about him. He'd come to regard her as a second mother figure and if she stayed in England he would feel she'd abandoned him. And she would miss him more than she dared think about just now. And as for Bernard... If their affair was over...

Her eyes misted over as she searched in her bag for a tissue to blow her nose.

One step at a time.

She felt a surge of apprehension as she paid the driver and looked up at the tall façade of the building that had been her home and workplace as a medical student and then a qualified doctor. It usually felt as if she was coming home again but this time was different.

* * *

'So, you'll get your exam results in a couple of weeks, I understand?' Don smiled across the desk at her. 'I was so relieved to get your email this week to say you were coming back to report on the course.'

'Thanks for your reply. I'm glad you were free to see me this morning.'

'I would have made time for you, Julia.' The consultant hesitated, running a hand through his steel-grey hair as he observed his star pupil. Something told him that she wasn't feeling her usual positive self.

'Would you like more coffee? You must be tired after your early start this morning.'

'No, thanks.'

She sat up straight against the back of her chair as she tried to brighten herself up. In the background she could hear the hum of the endless traffic outside on the forecourt of the hospital. An ambulance screeched to a halt and the siren stopped. It was weird. She should be feeling nostalgic by now.

'I've kept in touch with your progress over in France,' Don told her in a casual, friendly tone.

She managed a tight smile. 'I thought you might.'

'Oh, yes. I wasn't going to let you slip through my fingers. I've invested a lot in your training. Seen you grow up from student days. I'll be retiring soon, you know, well, in a couple of years.'

'No, I didn't know. You'll be missed here.'

'Oh, nobody is indispensable. Anyway, to go back to my progress reports from France, your professor, Bernard Cappelle, seems to think very highly of you. When I spoke to him a few days ago he told me you'd made excellent progress and he had high hopes for your exam results. From the way he spoke it seemed you might be staying on in France.'

Her heart gave a little leap of excitement but she remained silent, waiting for him to continue.

He carried on, wondering why she wasn't making any comment.

'That's why I'm so delighted to see you here in London today. There's the possibility of a promotion in the department, and then when I retire in two years my vacancy will be up for grabs. I've no doubt that, having excelled on the prestigious course at St Martin, you would be a strong candidate.'

He broke off. 'Julia, I think you should take a rest for a few hours to recover from the journey. I've asked Housekeeping to prepare your old room in the medics' quarters. My secretary has the keys. Let's meet up here in my office about four this afternoon.'

He stood and walked round the desk. She remembered how he'd been a father figure to her when she'd gone through the messy divorce days. He wasn't fooled by the brave face she was trying to effect. He held out his hand as she stood up, making a valiant effort to keep going.

She grasped his hand. 'Yes, you're quite right, a rest would be a good idea. I'll be back at four. Thanks, Don, for—'

'For treating you like one of my daughters.' He grinned. 'When you've got four girls at home you become an expert at sensing when something is not quite right.'

She smiled back, knowing she hadn't fooled him. She would have to sort out her problems, emotional and career-wise, before she came back.

She fell into a troubled sleep the moment her head hit the pillow. But the dreams that haunted her throughout were worse than being awake. She was dreaming that Philippe was seriously ill, that Bernard wasn't there with him, that he was on the island looking for her, calling her name, but she was calling out to him from the sea where she felt as if she was drowning. The water was over her head but her arms and legs weren't working properly… She managed to struggle up from the depths of her sleep. Relief flooded through her as she realised she was safe in her room. She was wide awake now and her mind had cleared. She knew she had to speak to Bernard as soon as possible.

He wasn't answering his phone. She tried several times. She'd get hold of Michel Devine in *Urgences*.

'Michel?'

'Michel Devine.'

His abrupt manner and the background noise told her he was on duty.

'It's Julia.'

'Ah, Julia. I thought you were in England. Bernard told me—'

'I'm trying to call him but he's not answering.'

'He's up in Paediatrics with Philippe—that's why he's not answering. I'll get a message to him if—'

'Is Philippe OK?'

'We're not sure. Bernard brought him in this morning. He's going through tests for meningitis.'

'Oh, no!'

'Don't worry, Julia. Philippe is in safe hands and Bernard is constantly with him at his bedside. What message shall I give Bernard?'

'Tell him…tell him I…tell him I'm coming back tonight. Thanks, Michel.'

* * *

She glanced at her watch as she zipped up her bag. Good thing she hadn't unpacked anything except her toothbrush. She went out into the corridor. She'd contacted Don, who'd agreed to see her earlier that afternoon.

He was waiting for her in his consulting room in Outpatients. A couple of patients were waiting outside as she went in and closed the door.

'Thanks for seeing me at such short notice. I'll make it brief because I know you've got patients waiting.'

'So why the change of plan, Julia?' He got up from his desk and moved over to the window where there were a couple of armchairs and a small table. 'Have you had any lunch?'

'I'll get something on the train.'

'The train?'

'I'm going back. Bernard Cappelle's son is ill with suspected meningitis. I have to be there with them. Sorry, Don, but it's put everything in perspective, coming back to England. I wasn't sure what it was I wanted but now I am.'

For a moment the consultant stared at her before he realised the reason behind her strange behaviour.

'Ah, I get the full picture now. I have to say I wondered if there was something going on between you and Bernard. So you're an item, to quote my daughters, are you?'

She hesitated. 'Yes, we've built up a relationship, a complicated relationship, and I don't know where it's going, but...' She stared across the small table at Don. 'I shouldn't be burdening you with all this.'

'Julia, you are talking to an expert in the affairs of the heart and in my opinion you've got it pretty bad. So I'm all agog to hear what you're going to do about it.'

She hesitated. 'I've got to think about it.'

'What's there to think about? You're obviously head over heels in love with the man. Call me an old romantic but you shouldn't turn your back on that sort of relationship.'

'But, Don, remember when I was going through that awful divorce and I told you I'd never trust my own judgement of character again? I was trying to be rational this time, taking my time to think through the problems of marrying Bernard and carrying on with my career.'

'You were too young when you married that obnoxious man. You'd had no experience of people like that. Now you're an extremely intelligent and experienced woman. I'm sad to see you going back because I had great plans for your future here. But you've got to go back and stay there with Bernard. You obviously love both him and his young son. Let me know as soon as the boy has been through all his tests at the hospital.'

The journey seemed much longer on the way back. She was amazed to see Michel Devine waiting for her at St Martin station. She'd told him the time her train from Calais–Frethun would arrive.

'How's Philippe?'

'Still having tests.' He opened the car door for her. 'Bernard is with him the whole time but the paediatric department is firmly in charge.'

'I just hope it's not meningitis.'

'If it is, he's in the best hospital to deal with it. And he's got the best father to lavish attention on him.'

'Thanks for picking me up, Michel.'

'I thought you might be shattered after going there and back in the space of a few hours. I thought of sending a taxi for you but I'm going off duty now and I can get you back to the hospital myself.'

'Well, it's much appreciated.'

'I'm so glad you've come back. You definitely belong over here…with Bernard. As a widower of three years, I was pleased when I saw you and Bernard getting on so well. A good relationship like yours is worth sticking to. My wife and I were only married for three years before she lost her battle with cancer. While she was alive were the happiest days of my life.'

She swallowed hard as she heard the raw emotion in his voice. They were drawing into the forecourt of the hospital.

'Thanks, Michel. I'll go straight up to Paediatrics.'

He switched off the engine and came round to help her out. 'I'll put your bag in Reception till you need it, then I'll go off duty.'

'Thanks for the advice.'

He gave her a sad smile. 'What advice?'

'Not in so many words but you nudged me in the right direction.'

'I hope so.'

CHAPTER THIRTEEN

JULIA pushed open the swing doors that led into the paediatric ward. It was late in the evening now and most of the children had been settled down for sleep. The lights had been dimmed in the main ward. She could see the ward sister walking towards her now.

'Ah, Caroline!'

She was glad they'd met socially during the summer. She also knew that she was one of the most experienced and well-qualified sisters in the hospital.

She began to relax. 'How is Philippe?'

Caroline frowned. 'I'm afraid the tests are still inconclusive. Bernard is with him. He's been here all day. I thought you were in England, Julia.'

'I made a brief visit to see the boss of my department. I'm back now. Change of plan. Where is…?'

'Let me take you to his room.'

Caroline took her to a room near the nurses' station. The door was slightly ajar. She pushed it open.

'A visitor for you, Bernard.'

He was sitting by Philippe's bed, hunched over his son, his head resting in his hands, his elbows on the sheet. He turned his head and for an instant she saw a flash of welcoming light in his eyes before the mask of total dejection returned.

'I thought you were in England.'

Sister went out and closed the door behind her as Julia approached the sick child's bed. Bernard stood up, running a hand through his dishevelled hair. She could see that he hadn't shaved that day. The dark stubble she'd noticed he always had in the mornings was now much more prominent— positively designer stubble, she couldn't help thinking. She longed to draw him against her and hold him there but sensed the cold aura surrounding him.

'I came back,' she said lamely. 'I was worried about Philippe.'

She leaned across the small patient now, automatically reaching for his pulse. It was racing along too fast, almost impossible to count the beats. His skin was dangerously hot.

'What's the latest?'

Bernard handed her the notes. She was still scanning the test results as one of the doctors on the paediatric firm came in.

'What's the latest news from Pathology, Thibault?' Bernard asked, his calm voice belying the obvious anxiety that cloaked the rest of him.

'A glimmer of hope, Bernard. The latest blood sample gave negative results for meningitis. I'm going to take another sample now.'

She stood beside Bernard as the blood sample was taken.

'It could be septicaemia, couldn't it?' he said to the young doctor as he prepared to return to the pathology laboratory.

'Or it could be the antibiotics beginning to kick in,' Julia said quietly, thinking out loud.

The three of them pooled their ideas, each anxious that the dreaded diagnosis of suspected meningitis should be proved to be wrong.

'We'll just have to hope, Bernard,' Dr. Thibault said gently. 'Tonight is the crucial time. As you know, if we don't have an improvement in your son's condition by tomorrow morning there is a chance that—'

'Yes, yes,' Bernard said, his voice wavering now. He didn't want to contemplate that his son's illness could be fatal. 'We can beat it! This is the twenty-first century and we'll pool our skills to save Philippe.'

'If I might suggest, Bernard,' the young doctor said, carefully, 'you've been here all day and you must be tired. I think I could arrange for you to take a break if you would approve of that?'

'I can't leave Philippe at this stage.'

'I'll call the path lab and ask them to collect this blood immediately. I can stay here with your son for the next hour.'

* * *

Julia looked across the small table at Bernard. The canteen had been deserted when they'd arrived but she had phoned the kitchen and the staff cook on night duty had turned up to prepare some food.

Chicken and vegetable soup had been placed in front of them, along with a crusty baguette heated up in the oven and a basket of fresh fruit—apples, oranges and bananas.

It wasn't until they'd started to eat the soup that they both realised how hungry they were.

'Did you have lunch over in England?'

She put down her spoon, having polished off her first helping. 'There wasn't time. I meant to get a sandwich on the train but I wasn't hungry. I'm hungry now.'

'There's more soup in this casserole,' Bernard said, dipping in with the soup ladle the waitress had left on the table.

It was only when she'd finished the last piece of her apple that her brain seemed to function again.

'Dr Thibault was quite right to send you off

for a break. You looked terrible when I first got here.'

'Thanks! You weren't looking your usual self either.' His eyes seemed to be boring into her. 'Care to tell me why you're here?'

'I told you; I was worried about Philippe.'

'And?'

'Bernard, I don't think we should talk about this until we've got through tonight.'

'We? You don't have to stay, Julia.'

'Oh, but I do. I can't rest until I know that… that he's out of danger.'

Bernard stood up. 'Neither can I.'

She must have dozed off in the high-backed arm-chair beside Philippe's bed. Bernard, at the other side, was wide awake, she could see, sponging his son's chest with cold water.

As he dabbed it dry he looked across at her. 'The rash isn't so pronounced. It's disappearing in places. I'm beginning to hope it's septi-caemia.'

'Still dangerous,' Julia said quietly. 'But easier to treat than meningitis.'

Bernard nodded. 'He's opening his eyes… Julia!'

She jumped up from the chair and went round the bed. 'Philippe?'

'Where am I?'

Julia could feel tears of joy pricking her eyes as she heard the weak little voice. A tear trickled down her cheek as she leaned over Philippe, taking hold of his tiny hand. She'd been right to come back here. This was where she belonged.

Philippe was propped up against the pillows, eating a small carton of yoghurt. It was what he'd asked for as soon as he'd begun to feel stronger. Since the amazing recovery in the early morning he'd gradually gathered strength. The diagnosis was confirmed, septicaemia. His treatment and medication had been adjusted accordingly and there was every chance now that he was going to have a full recovery within days.

'Papa, can we go home? I want to see the cows.

Gaston will need some help with the milking today.'

'We'll need to stay here for another night at least.'

'But you'll both stay with me, won't you? Julia, you can stay, can't you? You won't leave me, will you?'

She looked at the anxious eyes of this young boy who meant so much to her and across the bed to his father whom she loved more than she'd ever imagined possible.

What would she do if he didn't want her any more?

CHAPTER FOURTEEN

SHE'D spent the night in the guest room. On Bernard's instructions Gaston had moved another bed into Philippe's room before they'd all arrived back from the hospital yesterday. Bernard had insisted she get a good night's sleep.

'You've spent the last three nights in an armchair so you must get a proper rest tonight,' he'd told her.

She'd argued that so had he. They could take turns at caring for Philippe during the night.

But Bernard had been adamant that he wanted to do the night watch. As she pulled the curtains fully back and fixed the ties, she raised her face to the morning sun. There was little heat now in the late autumnal rays but it was soothing to her nerves. Bernard had been right. She did need a good rest. Her nerves had been totally frazzled over the last few days since Philippe had become ill.

And the journey to London and back had tired her more than usual. Well, the discussion with Don Grainger had set her thinking.

She sighed as she looked out over the garden. The fallen leaves on the lawn. The roses drooping and waiting to be dead-headed. She'd pushed the emotional problems that still existed between Bernard and herself to the back of her mind until they were absolutely sure Philippe was out of danger. And she didn't want a discussion while Philippe was the main priority in Bernard's life.

Maybe she should simply go back to her room in the medics' quarters at St Martin? Marianne and Gaston were taking care of all the practicalities of the situation. Was she really needed here?

'Julia, I've brought you some coffee.'

She raced to the door at the welcome sound of Bernard's voice.

He was standing outside in the corridor, carrying a small tray, the expression on his face totally unreadable.

'How's Philippe?'

'He had a good night. In fact, so did I. I slept until Marianne brought the coffee tray just now. She's taken over to give me a break. I feel that now Philippe is out of danger and you're back from London we should talk. My place or yours?'

For the first time for days he looked relaxed again. There was a half-smile on his face but still that awkward coolness that had to be resolved if she was to convince him that she'd made a mistake in returning to London without discussing it with him first.

She'd had time to think and she knew that she wanted Bernard on any terms. She could be happy with him without them marrying or having a child of their own. Philippe felt like her own child already and if Bernard didn't want more children, neither did she. But did he want her? Had the short-term affair been enough for him to decide to go back to his independent lifestyle?

She moved towards him. 'Which room would you prefer?'

'I'd like to install myself back in my bedroom so let's go there. I need to shave and everything is in my bathroom. We can talk while I'm in there before I arrange my schedule at the hospital for today. I plan to go in for a couple of hours this morning. I've arranged for a nurse to come out from the hospital to be with Philippe, and Marianne and Gaston will be in charge here.'

She followed behind him. This wasn't how she'd planned to discuss her change of heart—in a bathroom!

He held the tray in one hand and pushed open his door with the other, walking swiftly over to the small round table by the window. She sank down into one of the armchairs and watched as he poured the coffee into the cups. He took a sip and swallowed. 'Mmm, that first coffee taste of the morning. Nothing like it!'

She watched, mesmerised, as he began to walk towards the bathroom, the cup firmly clenched in his fingers.

'Bernard! You're not really going to shave while we have the most important discussion of our lives!'

He turned, a half-smile again on his face. 'Ah, so you do have something to tell me? Don said you might have.'

He moved swiftly back to the table and stretched his long legs out in the armchair across from her.

'Don?'

'Who else knows you almost as well as I do? Well, professionally anyway. He phoned me last night to check how Philippe was but also to fill me in about your discussions. He said he thought you would be staying in France and conceded that his loss was my gain. He'd hoped to guide you up the career ladder in London until his retirement and he was sad to lose you.'

'So you were simply talking professionally?'

'What else?'

She was beginning to feel alarmed. The two men who'd been most influential in her career had been discussing her.

'He didn't touch on anything…er…well, personal?'

He feigned surprise at her question. 'Such as?'

'Oh, Bernard, you can be so infuriating at times!'

She leapt out of her seat and went across so she would have the advantage of looking down at him. 'Such as whether our relationship was over or not?'

'Ah, that.' He half rose from his seat and pulled her down onto his lap. 'Well, he might have mentioned it.'

She turned her head and looked up at him. He had the advantage now and she'd really wanted a discussion. She needed to convince him that she'd come to the right decision at last.

'I've had time to think over the last few days,' she said quietly. 'I know you don't want another child but I've realised that I can live as a surgeon so long as I have you…and Philippe, of course… in my life. I don't need a baby any more.'

'But I do,' he replied gently, drawing her so close that she could feel his heart beating. 'I've known for some time now that, contrary to how I used to feel, I would love to have a baby… but only with you. I've watched you caring for Philippe and I realised that you would be the most wonderful mother to our baby.'

'So why didn't you tell me you'd had a change of heart?'

'I wanted to be sure you wouldn't choose to have a baby with me just because I could fulfil one of your dearest wishes. I had to be sure that you loved me as much as I love you.'

'But I thought that was obvious!' She put her hands against his cheeks and drew his lips against hers.

She felt his response deepening, his hands gently caressing her body. Gently, he lifted her up into his arms and carried her over to the bed.

'Can I make my love any more obvious?' she whispered as they both lay back, exhausted by their lovemaking and panting for breath.

She turned her head on the pillow to look at him as she curled her toes against his, one of the positions she loved to adopt after they'd made love.

He smiled. 'I think you've convinced me… But, then again, I just might be having doubts.'

He rested on his elbow, looking down into her eyes. 'I'll need convincing often if we're going to stay together for the rest of our lives.'

She gazed up into his face. 'And are we going to stay together for the rest of our lives?'

Before she realised what he was doing he was on his knees beside the bed, looking up at her with those devastatingly sexy eyes that were expressing the love he felt for her.

'Julia, will you marry me?'

His voice was husky, full of emotion as he asked her the question she'd thought he might never ask. She'd had her doubts before but now that they'd sorted out the problems that had been holding them back she was free to commit herself.

She leaned forward and put her hands over his. 'Of course I will.'

He was in bed beside her, drawing her into his arms. 'Oh, Julia, my love…'

'Bernard, the nurse is here to look after Philippe.'

Julia struggled up through the tangle of sheets as she heard Marianne's voice outside in the corridor. She swung her legs over the side of the bed.

Bernard put out a restraining hand. 'I'll go,' he whispered. 'Stay here and rest. There's no hurry. Take your time before you come downstairs.'

He was smiling fondly down at her. 'As soon as Marianne hears our news, you'll need all your energy to cope with her. She'll be thinking ahead to the wedding and all the plans that will be needed.'

'Please don't tell her till I come downstairs.'

His smile broadened. 'I won't need to. That woman is psychic, I'm sure. She's been expecting an announcement ever since you stayed that first night here.'

It was only as she climbed out of the bath and reached for a towel a little later that she realised the enormity of the tasks ahead of her. There were phone calls to make to her parents—that must be a priority. How would her mother take it? Last time she'd announced she was going to be married her mother had been very unsure. She'd gone ahead with it defiantly and had lived to regret it. But this time she was absolutely sure of her man.

But the practicalities had to be dealt with. Where would they have the wedding? France? England? There'd have to be a long list of guests. How much easier if would be if they could just sneak away, the three of them.

As she thought of the three of them making a real family unit at last she felt a great longing to see her soon-to-be stepchild as soon as possible.

Hurrying along to his room, she slowed down to check that she was presentable. It was still early but so much had happened, so much had been resolved and so much needed to be sorted out. As her mother would say, she should gather her wits about her.

Yes, there would be a nurse from the hospital

taking care of Philippe and she didn't want to look as if she'd been rolling about in Bernard's bed all night. It had only been this morning when she'd given herself completely to the joy of being finally sure that their future was well and truly together.

She smiled as she recognised one of the nurses from Paediatrics. 'Hello, Florence.'

'Julia!' Philippe's voice was croaky and weak but his happiness at seeing her again was expressed in the way he held out his thin little arms towards her.

She leaned down and clasped him against her. 'Oh, Philippe, it's good to see you looking so much better.'

'Can I come down and have breakfast with you and Papa? I'm feeling hungry now.'

'You said you didn't want to eat anything,' Florence said gently. 'Let me bring something up from the kitchen for you. I don't think you're strong enough to go downstairs yet.'

As if on cue, Bernard chose that moment to come in. 'What's this about breakfast, Philippe?'

He reached down and picked up his small son in his arms. Julia grabbed a blanket from the end of the bed and wrapped it round him. He snuggled happily against his father.

'Take a break, Florence,' Bernard said. 'Come down and have some breakfast with us. The more the merrier around the table today!'

Marianne was waiting for them in the kitchen, cafetière in her hand. The delicious smell of coffee had wafted up the stairs as Julia had walked behind Bernard, followed by Florence. Julia sat down beside Bernard, as close as she could to Philippe so that she could make sure he was comfortable in Bernard's arms. She doubted he would eat much, if anything, after the ordeal he'd been through, but it was the experience of being once more part of the family that he needed.

Their family! Her heart seemed to turn over at the implications of what was happening.

What a momentous occasion. Was Bernard going to make an announcement here at the breakfast table? With Florence here the news would spread like wildfire at the hospital. Was that what he wanted?

She glanced up at him as he cleared his throat. He was looking oh, so pleased with himself, happiness oozing from every fibre of his muscular, athletic, tantalisingly sexy body. His happiness was infectious. There was a feeling of total unreality about the situation but she'd never felt as happy as she did at that moment. Yes, she wanted to tell the whole world that she was soon to be married to the most wonderful man on the planet.

'Come and sit down, Marianne,' Bernard said. 'I want everybody here because I've got an announcement to make. Where's Gaston?'

'He's just finished the milking. He's going to take a shower as soon as—'

'Ask him to come in here, Marianne, if he's still out there, taking off his boots.'

Gaston glanced around the table as he walked in, treading carefully across the room in his socks to sit next to his wife.

'I haven't even washed my hands,' he complained to his wife before looking across at Bernard. 'What's this all about? I need to clean up.'

'Julia has just consented to become my wife. I want you all to share in our happiness.'

'And about time too,' Gaston said, now grinning from ear to ear. 'Creeping around in the middle of the night when the two of you—'

'Gaston!' his wife hissed at him. 'Be quiet.'

'No, I won't be quiet. This is the best news we've had in this house since I came to work here and told you that Marianne had set a date for our wedding.'

'And that was a long time ago, wasn't it, Gaston? I was much younger but I remember it well because my father opened one of his special bottles of champagne so we could drink a toast. I haven't been down to the cellar recently. Do you know if there's still a bottle of that vintage?'

Gaston struggled to his feet. 'I checked a few weeks ago because I was hoping you'd get a move on, Bernard. Shall I put a bottle on ice?'

'Bring a couple. We'll have a glass now and

drink some more this evening when we can all relax at the end of the day.'

'Julia, are you going to be my new mother?' Philippe asked shyly.

She swallowed hard. 'I'm going to be Papa's wife. You can carry on calling me Julia because I'll never replace your real mother, will I?'

'I suppose not. Well, you can be my second mother, then, but I'd like to still call you Julia.'

Gaston arrived with the champagne. 'It's freezing cold down there in the cellar. I've brought the ice bucket but we don't really need it. And it needs polishing. Hasn't been used for years. I cleared away the cobwebs but...'

He glanced across at his wife, who was already holding a duster.

Julia gathered Philippe into her arms as Bernard stood to do the honours. The cork was expertly removed with barely a hiss, the champagne was poured, the glasses raised.

Marianne was in tears now that she'd got the situation she'd hoped for. It was almost too much for her as she raised her glass to the happy pair.

'Congratulations!' she said, through her tears.

Florence was overwhelmed at being the first to acknowledge that there was some truth in the rumours that had been circulating in the hospital. Just wait until she got back there at the end of the week!

'Well, that all went very well today,' Bernard said, as he climbed into bed. 'Do you think you could put that list down and give me some attention? There can't be that much to do when you're organising a wedding, can there?'

'You must be joking! Not for the groom perhaps. So long as you write a good speech and…'

'Oh, do I have to give a speech? I'd better start now, then. Just lend me that notepad you're still scribbling in.'

He reached across and grabbed it from her, glancing down as he did so. 'Oh, how did your mother take the news?'

'Very well, actually. I gathered that you'd phoned Don this morning and he'd phoned Mum to prepare her for the news. They're old friends from way back at medical school. He'd also given you a very good character reference, I believe, because she said she was looking forward to meeting you.'

'And did you agree on where the wedding should take place?'

'The church where my grandmother and my mother were married in Montreuil sur Mer. I was baptised there because my mother insisted on keeping our French family connection going.'

'So, a very interesting family choice.'

'And do you approve?'

'Absolutely!' He drew her into his arms. 'Is that all the business for the day completed? The night nurse has taken over from Florence in Philippe's room so we're free to go to sleep or...'

As she gave herself up to the delights of their lovemaking she knew she was going to be the happiest bride ever.

EPILOGUE

THE day of the wedding dawned with a flurry of snowflakes drifting outside the window. Julia had spent the night in a hotel in the village with her parents in line with the tradition of not seeing her groom before the wedding. It had been hard to be separated from Bernard but as he'd reminded her when he kissed her goodnight it was only one night apart and then they would be together for the rest of their lives.

After Julia had eaten breakfast in bed, her mother arrived with Claudine, the dressmaker, and Monique, a hairdresser who was going to shampoo and arrange her long blonde hair so that it would fall over her shoulders underneath the delicate lace veil.

Claudine was going to dress her and make sure that the stunning silk dress they'd designed between them was shown off to perfection. The dressmaker held out the stiff petticoat and Julia stepped into it, one hand on Claudine's shoulder to steady herself. It looked gorgeous!

The ladies in the room asked for her to give them a twirl. She obliged. It didn't feel at all stiff and starchy as she'd thought it might.

Finally, she stood in front of the mirror fully dressed in the superbly beautiful dress while her mother, Claudine and Monique stood around to admire her. Behind her reflection she could see her mother wiping away a tear. She turned and hugged her.

Her mother hugged her back, but gently. 'Careful of your dress, darling. I'm so happy for you. This time you're going to be very happy.'

And as she walked into the church on her father's arm she knew she really was going to be happy for the rest of her life. She'd chosen and been chosen by the most wonderful man in the world.

Walking down the aisle, she felt like a fairy-tale princess on her way to marry her prince. He was there in front of the altar, her own Prince Charming. He turned as she was nearing him, his eyes shining with love and admiration at this vision of perfection, his soon-to-be wife.

As she reached his side she realised there was someone else with her in front of the altar. Glancing down, she saw Philippe smiling up at her. He'd left his place in the procession of bridesmaids behind her and come to join her and his father. He looked adorable in his tailor-made suit.

'Let him stay with us,' she whispered to Bernard, who smiled and nodded in agreement.

The organist stopped playing. The congregation fell silent. The marriage service began.

There was another flurry of snowflakes as they came out of the church and stood on the steps for the photographs. Julia and Bernard smiled for the cameras. Her parents joined them with her brothers and their families. Philippe joined them and then agreed to leave the bridal pair to join Julia's parents, who were going to take him back to the farm. The photo shoot would have gone on longer but the descending snow put an end to that.

'The kiss!' everyone was calling out.

Bernard took her in his arms and they kissed to loud shouts of approval.

'Encore! Another kiss!'

'Just one more,' Bernard whispered. 'I want you all to myself now.'

As soon as they could get away into the car, they did so.

'See you back at the farm,' Bernard called out to everybody as he drove away. He'd insisted on going against tradition by driving his own car over to the church so that they could be really alone on the way back home.

'I wanted you to myself for the first few minutes of our marriage,' he said, pulling the car in behind a tractor on the narrow country lane. 'I'm taking a short cut, which should be quicker than the main road so we'll be back at the farm before our guests arrive, I hope. We'll have to be sociable for the rest of the day.'

She smiled. 'It's been such a whirlwind of organisation for the last few weeks. I'll be so glad to have some normal married life.'

'Do you think we'll ever have a normal married life, whatever that is?'

'I know we're both continuing with our careers but as we both understand what the other's going through we can pull together, help each other...until we have a baby, when it might get a bit harder.'

She glanced across at him. His eyes were on the narrow road ahead. The tractor had turned into a gate and left the road clear at last. The snowflakes had stopped now and the pale wintry sun was peeping out from behind a cloud.

He changed gear as they went down into the valley where he could see smoke spiralling from the farm chimneys. 'I wonder when that will be?'

'Well, it could be sooner than we expected. I promised I would tell you if...well, don't get too excited but I'm seven days late.'

'My darling! Why didn't you tell me?'

'I'm telling you now! But it could just be the

excitement of the wedding and all the preparations. Don't, for heaven's sake, start getting your
hopes up.'

He pulled into the farmyard and switched the
engine off.

'Come here, you gorgeous girl, my wonderful bride.'

He kissed her gently on the lips. As his kiss
deepened she moved in his arms.

'Later, darling. Our guests are arriving.'

'Keep me informed, won't you?' he whispered
as a car pulled in behind them.

'Of course.' She smiled happily as Gaston
opened a door for her to climb out. A long strip
of red carpet had been laid in front of her leading
to the kitchen door. Bernard was already there
for her holding out his hand to guide her indoors.

Bernard's speech was hilarious. Everybody was
still laughing as they raised their glasses for another toast. They were all crowded into the dining room, the food spread out as a buffet.

'There's more food in the kitchen, Julia,'

Marianne said quietly. 'Shall I bring the desserts yet?'

'I'll tell everybody the desserts are in the kitchen when they would like to help themselves. Nobody's standing on ceremony here. Everybody seems to be getting on well.'

'I should think so,' Gaston said, topping up her wine glass. 'Good thing we've got plenty of bottles in the cellar.'

She moved through the guests, trying to have a word with everybody. They all complimented her on her dress, especially her cousin Chantal. They'd been great friends as children and nothing ever changed when they met up again.

'Your dress is absolutely gorgeous, Julia! It fits you perfectly.'

'I had it made in Montreuil by the daughter of the dressmaker who made the wedding dresses of our grandmother and my mother, who's over there looking very happy to be the mother of the bride, don't you think?'

'She's also happy to be chatting to my mother. You can tell they're twins. They're so alike, aren't they? And they don't see enough of each other nowadays so they never stop talking when they do meet!'

'Just like we do!'

They both laughed.

Chantal turned back to admire Julia again. 'You're so slim. That dress fits you like a glove.'

'I suppose I am…at the moment.' Now, why had she said that? Was it because Chantal had always been more like a sister when they'd been small? The antidote to all those brothers bossing her around?

Chantal moved nearer and put a hand on her arm, guiding her through the throng of guests to a small window seat where they could whisper together. 'You're not…? Are you?'

Julia smiled. 'Maybe. Too early to say but I hope so.'

'So do I! Please remember me when you're choosing godparents.'

'Chantal, you would be my first choice! I'm so glad we're going to see more of each other now that I'm going to be living in France. It's easy for you to come over from Paris by train, isn't it?'

'I may be coming back to this area sooner than you think. I've split up with Jacques.'

'No! But I thought you two had the most perfect relationship.'

'So did I. He's gone back to his wife. He'd managed to fool me completely for a whole year. I didn't realise I was his mistress. I felt such a fool when he told me.'

'So are you thinking of leaving the hospital?'

'I've left! Couldn't stand working alongside him when all the time—'

Chantal broke off as Bernard arrived.

'Not interrupting anything, am I?'

'No! Well, actually Chantal was just telling me she's leaving Paris and moving back to this area.'

'I'll be looking for a job, Bernard. Any vacancies for a well-qualified and experienced doctor?'

'Send me your CV and I'll see what I can do, Chantal.'

'I'll do that!'

Philippe came running across the room to join them. 'Papa, I've got an idea. You see my friend Jules over there with his parents? Well, he got a little brother during the summer. Now that Julia and you are married, does that mean I can have a baby brother or sister? Maybe as a Christmas present?'

He was looking up beseechingly now at Julia.

She looked across at Bernard, who was smiling happily. 'We'll have to see what happens, won't we?' he told his son. 'These things take time.'

Philippe looked pleased. Papa hadn't ruled the idea out. He ran back to his friend Jules to say he might get a baby brother or sister but probably not for Christmas.

'These things take time,' he told Jules airily.

'I didn't think they would stay so late,' Julia said as she slipped into bed beside Bernard.

'Sign of a good party! I'd say it was a huge success.'

'It was wonderful to see my parents and all

three of my brothers again but I'm glad they're staying at the hotel in the village, otherwise we'd still be downstairs, having supper.'

'Today has been a wonderful day!' he said, drawing her against him.

'It's been the happiest day of my life. Wasn't Philippe sweet when he asked for a baby brother? I don't know about Christmas but he might get one for his birthday!'

'Wonder woman!'

She laughed.

Bernard drew her closer. 'Just one request.'

'Yes?'

'You're not going to leave me in the early morning and go to the guest room, are you?'

'Not now that you've made an honest woman of me.'

'Any regrets?'

She sighed as she felt his arms drawing her even closer.

'Only that we didn't get together like this sooner.'

'You mean like this…or like this…or like this…?'

She laughed. 'You know what I mean.'

'I certainly do…'

* * * * *

November

December

January

Mills & Boon® Large Print
Medical

February

SYDNEY HARBOUR HOSPITAL: AVA'S RE-AWAKENING	Carol Marinelli
HOW TO MEND A BROKEN HEART	Amy Andrews
FALLING FOR DR FEARLESS	Lucy Clark
THE NURSE HE SHOULDN'T NOTICE	Susan Carlisle
EVERY BOY'S DREAM DAD	Sue MacKay
RETURN OF THE REBEL SURGEON	Connie Cox

March

HER MOTHERHOOD WISH	Anne Fraser
A BOND BETWEEN STRANGERS	Scarlet Wilson
ONCE A PLAYBOY…	Kate Hardy
CHALLENGING THE NURSE'S RULES	Janice Lynn
THE SHEIKH AND THE SURROGATE MUM	Meredith Webber
TAMED BY HER BROODING BOSS	Joanna Neil

April

A SOCIALITE'S CHRISTMAS WISH	Lucy Clark
REDEEMING DR RICCARDI	Leah Martyn
THE FAMILY WHO MADE HIM WHOLE	Jennifer Taylor
THE DOCTOR MEETS HER MATCH	Annie Claydon
THE DOCTOR'S LOST-AND-FOUND HEART	Dianne Drake
THE MAN WHO WOULDN'T MARRY	Tina Beckett